Academy of Sorcery

Term 1: The Unleashing Trials

Alexa B. James

&

Athena Phoenix

Academy of Sorcery, Term 1: The Unleashing Trials
© 2019 Alexa B. James & Athena Phoenix

Published in the United States by Speak Now.

Cover Design by Melody Simmons.

First edition
ISBN-13: 978-1-945780-77-6

BLURB

Magic is dangerous.

I should know. It got me a thirty-year sentence scrubbing toilets for a scumbag wizard.

My only hope is the Unleashing, a ceremony that unlocks the dormant powers of magical descendants when we turn eighteen. Since my mom was a lowly psychic, I don't expect to be blessed with much more than the ability to forecast the weather.

But when the sorcerers unlock my magic, all hell breaks loose. Turns out, I'm not a wizard, witch, or even a sorcerer. I'm...*something else.*

Because of my unique abilities, I'm required to attend the Academy of Sorcery until I learn to harness and control my magic. Not only that, but the three sexiest and most powerful sorcerers on campus are assigned to guard me night and day. Jackpot, right?

Not quite.

Turns out these guys aren't too happy with the arrangement, and they show it by making my life hell. That's just the beginning of my troubles. The mean-girl squad declares open season on me, a mysterious woman attacks me every time I step off campus, and my professor is too hot for his own good. And when it's time to find a weapon to help me master my abilities, my magic chooses...a *spork.*

It's going to be a long year.

Good thing I've got what it takes to survive it.

Chapter 1

"Magic is dangerous, Jade," Dad says, his arms crossed over his skinny chest. "For your sake, I hope you don't have any."

I pull two pieces of toast from the ancient contraption on the counter. Burnt again.

"I know, Dad," I say, though I can't share his hope. Magic is the one thing that could get me out of this life.

"Should you really chance going to the Unleashing at all?" Dad frets. "Silas won't be happy with you leaving during a workday."

As I set down a jar of grape jelly next to my chipped plate on the counter, I glance out the window at the rain falling outside. Despite the weather, for the first time in a long time, there's a small spark of hope inside me today.

It's a big day for anyone who could have some type of magic lurking inside. Since my mom was a psychic, my family is marked as one that carries magic. That means that today, my luck could change.

Reminding myself to keep looking on the bright side, I scrape off the brown part from each slice of toast and shake the crumbs into the sink.

Today is *the* day. The one thing I've been looking forward to since Mom died two years ago.

Dad turns on the tiny television set sitting on the counter. The local weather report blares through the small kitchen, talking about the most recent hurricane that has swept through Florida. Damage we're used to with the crazy weather in Jacksonville in this age of almost weekly natural disasters. Apparently there was a time when Florida was a tourist destination, but I wasn't alive for that. Today, it's half covered in water, infested with mosquitos and vultures, and rife with crime by both humans and supernaturals.

"I think you should sit out the Unleashing."

Even from the other side of the room, I can feel Dad's worried gaze tugging at me. Of course he's nervous for the

Term 1: Unleashing Trials

Unleashing of Magic ceremony today. I can't really blame the guy for being scared of magic, since the courts blamed Mom's magic for the death of Silas's wife six years ago. Silas. Shit. If I'm late again, he will not be happy. I can hear the ticking of the clock all the way across our crappy two-bedroom rental, reminding me I'm late for the job I inherited from Mom. I grab my toast and turn to Dad.

"I want to go," I say. "Not to mention the fact that it's a requirement for magical descendants who have turned eighteen."

My birthday was last week, thank god. Seriously, I'm praying to whatever deity rules the universe that I have some badass powers. Maybe somehow it can get me out of the slave contract I'm bound to for basically the rest of my life.

"There are so many magical families invited. Who will even know if you don't go?"

"Probably no one," I admit. But I have the invitation the Society of Supernaturals sent me tucked safely in my pocket just in case.

Blowing out a breath, I smile at Dad. As frustrating as his stance on this is, I can't be angry. He's worried about me, the way he worries about everything.

Ever since Mom died in a freak accident on her way home from work, he's half the person he used to be. He quit his decent paying job to work from home. I can't even remember the last time I got him to leave the house. Hell, I'm surprised he's even trying to fight me on this point. But I have to admit he's right about my boss. Silas probably won't let me go.

God, just the mention of the warlock's name—the man who owns the next thirty-four years of my life—makes me all ragey inside.

Before I can take another bite of my toast, the clock starts to chime from the other room. I'm running late. That is *so* not what I need on a day when I'm asking Silas for a favor.

"Gotta go, Dad," I say as I grab my bag off the kitchen counter.

Dad looks at me with his sad, grey eyes, his shoulders slumping in defeat. My dad is... Fragile. I don't know what he'd do without me. After losing everything—our family and finances—he and I are all we have left.

But today, that could all change. Today, I could have *magic*.

Probably not, though. The chances of having magic are slim, since my dad has none and my mom was a psychic, which is not exactly the shining star of the magical world.

Reaching my arms around my dad's frail frame, I hug him gently. "Love you, Dad."

"I love you, too. Please be careful."

"Always."

After a short drive to Silas's estate, I pull into the drive and shut off the engine. Glancing out the windshield at the rain pouring over my old sedan, I let out a sigh, gathering the courage to ask Silas to let me go to the ceremony.

Once kids from magical families turn eighteen, we're required to go to the Unleashing Ceremony. That's when we're deemed responsible enough to wield our powers, even if they are only the ability to foresee the next earthquake. Until then, no one knows if we have magic, and if so, what kind and how much. All magical families are required to register their children with the Society of Supernaturals at birth, when a sorcerer comes to bind up any potential magic so no toddler can blow up his parents in a fit of rage, and middle schoolers can't give each other zits. Stuff like that. Though, if you ask me, that would have come in handy at my middle school.

But basically, anybody who has magic needs to learn to wield it safely, so they built academies to teach mastery of whatever branch of magic we might possess. Only powerful sorcerers can unleash the magic bound inside us, though. If they don't unleash it, it would just sit inside a person forever, unused and unknown.

I wonder if I have some hidden potential just lurking inside me. Maybe the potential to turn Silas into a toad if he doesn't let me go to the Unleashing. Though if he won't, all that potential will be wasted. Too bad.

With that thought in mind, I grab my bag and sprint for the back door, rain pouring over my head and soaking my long, blonde hair. I knock on the entrance, and Silas's butler opens the door.

"Good morning, Jade." Robert ushers me inside the kitchen. He's a sweet older vampire, probably turned in his late sixties, though it's anyone's guess how old he actually is. Poor guy got stuck working for Silas, too.

I peel off my soaked raincoat and hang it on a coat rack on the wall.

"Best get to work," Robert says. "Silas is in a mood today."

"Did you see it outside?" I gesture to the window. "I had to take an alternative route because of the flooding."

Robert offers a sympathetic smile. "You know he'll only see that as an excuse, even if it's true."

"The bastard." I go to the closet where all my cleaning supplies are, then look at the calendar hanging on the inside of the wooden door. Bathrooms.

Super. There are few tasks I loathe more than cleaning the man's nasty toilets.

Grabbing a basket, I load in my supplies and make my way to the stairs. This time of day, Silas is usually gone, but as it's the day of the Unleashing, I'm sure he's here just to make sure I don't try and sneak out. Which believe me, I've considered. If I didn't think he'd take it out on my poor dad, who's been through enough, I would.

I doubt they'll notice if I don't show up, but my family is a bit infamous because of my mom, so it's possible. Apparently even if you're trying to protect your daughter, you can't use your magical abilities to interfere with fate. That little slip, when my mom told my sister that a powerful judge named Silas was going to kill her, didn't prevent my sister's death. In fact, it only made my sister and her boyfriend decide to go after Silas and make sure that never happened.

In the fight, both Silas's wife and my sister were killed. Since my sister had attacked a man with "no provocation," and since Silas was of such high standing with the supernatural courts, he got off without so much as a warning. My mom, who had set those events in motion, was found to be responsible for all of it.

Instead of a death sentence, Silas gave my mom a life sentence—work as his servant for the next forty years, one year for every year his wife had lived before her murder. With a choice between that and death, my mom took what basically amounted to a life of slavery. Unfortunately, the terms of the contract said that her children would have to serve her term if she didn't. After six years of working for Silas, Mom died, leaving me thirty-four long years to serve out her contract.

With a bucket in one hand and a plunger in the other, I take the back stairs to the basement, doing my best to avoid places he might be lurking. There are two bathrooms down here, so I might be able to stay out of his way for a while.

Stepping off the last stair, I turn on the lights and find Silas sitting in the corner.

What a creep.

He crosses his legs and leers at me. "You're late, young lady. I'll be docking your pay for that."

"As is your right," I say through a forced smile. Trying to hold my tongue is a chore in itself, but as I learned a long time ago, arguing with him is a waste of breath. And maybe this once, if I'm polite, he'll be generous.

My nerves are in full-fledged explosion mode when I realize that now I'm going to have to ask him for a favor. I swallow down my fears and measure my words carefully before speaking.

Here goes nothing.

"So, the Unleashing is today," I begin. "As you know, I turned eighteen last week. I received my invitation in the mail. Here, see?" I pull the folded letter from my pocket and hold it out to him. "Since every descendant of magic has to go, that includes me. I need to take a few hours off work. It's not for me. It's the law."

But then, Silas thinks he's above the law. He glares as he stands from the chair. His 5-foot-8 frame isn't intimidating whatsoever, but he uses his position of power in the magic-wielder community to its fullest. The dude takes little man syndrome to a whole new level.

He snatches the letter from my hand, shakes his head, and rips the paper into pieces before dropping it to the floor.

If my mouth weren't hanging open in shock and indignation, I'd seriously have to bite my tongue not to give him a piece of my mind.

"You are a servant," he says in a cutting tone. "Not a witch. Even if you have magic, which I highly doubt, you are no longer free." He crosses his arms over his chest. "I own the next thirty-plus years of your life, and therefore I own your magic for that duration. I decide if and when you stay or go. You're lucky I allow you to live with your ailing father at all. If I weren't such a compassionate man, you would be living in my servants' quarters."

Compassionate man, my ass.

Term 1: Unleashing Trials

We both know that the only reason I get to live at home is because the courts granted my mother that right in her contract. I take a breath and do everything in my power to keep my mouth shut. Calling him out will only piss him off, and next thing you know, I'll be scrubbing the floor with a toothbrush for his amusement.

"Your life is mine," Silas purrs in a voice that makes my skin crawl. "Now take your supplies and get to cleaning my toilets. That's the work you deserve, and the work you'll do until you've paid off the debt your dead mother owed me."

He turns and disappears up the stairs. My gaze drops to the floor where the shredded invitation lies scattered across the carpet—along with my hopes and dreams. I let out a sigh and crouch to pick them up. He could have at least let me go to the Unleashing as a formality, even if I don't have magic. Now I'll probably have some supernatural law enforcement knocking on my door in a few weeks and handing me a fine for not showing up.

"Fuck my life," I mutter, crumpling the paper scraps. I head toward the bathroom, drop them into the toilet and watch as they spin in circles, disappearing down the drain.

There goes that. Brushing off my hands, I pull on the blue plastic gloves, pull out the cleaning supplies, and arrange them on the floor. Starting with the sink, I clean and polish, then move on to the toilet. Spray, scrub, hold my breath.

As I scrub, my mind conjures the image of Silas turning into a toad. Too bad I can't flush him down the toilet. I was an idiot to think Silas would allow me to go anywhere. Now I'll never know if I have magic at all. All that wasted toad-transforming potential.

Just when I'm starting to sweat from the scrubbing, and I'm elbow deep in the toilet, I hear voices outside the bathroom. Voices I don't recognize. Silas doesn't usually bring visitors down to where I'm cleaning, so I pause to swipe blonde hair off my forehead with the back of my wrist and strain to make out their voices. If Silas has to bring his guests all the way down here so they won't be overheard by anyone upstairs, it must be good.

"Look what you've been hiding," says a gruff voice from behind me. "This is a reportable offense, Silas."

I turn to find two of the most beautiful men I've ever seen standing behind my boss. Great. I'm in toilet water, and these two look like they've just stepped out of an ad for *Supernatural GQ*. The one who spoke has thick, luscious honey-blond hair that falls over his forehead, a strong square jaw, and just the barest hint of a dimple carved into his chiseled chin. His blue eyes are locked on me, studying me so closely I'm sure he can tell that his deep, growly voice does something indecent to my body.

"Quite the contrary, Rocco," Silas says, interrupting my admiration of the guy. My boss wrings his hands as he speaks. "Jade is my servant by law. Her life belongs to me. I have a contract."

"Silas." The other man stares him down from a height that must be nearly six and a half feet. His hair is so black it glints blue in the fluorescent light of the bathroom, and his broad shoulders speak of many, many hours at the gym. "You are a member of the Society. You know all eighteen-year-olds of magical descent must go through the Unleashing. That is the law, and it supersedes your contract." His lip gives a slight curl of distaste at the last word, and I know he must have heard about Silas's unconventional rulings as judge—and he doesn't approve.

"Maybe so, Thorn. But…"

"Enough," Thorn says, turning to me. "Stand up, girl."

My gaze flickers between the two of them. I have no clue who they are, but I'm intrigued. I hadn't expected the supernatural police to be so... Hot.

On the other hand, who the hell does this guy think he is, calling me *girl*? If they came to find me, they must know my name.

Rocco snaps his fingers at me. "On your feet, Cinderella."

With a huff, I get to my feet and plant my hands on my hips. Even if he's summoning me in the same manner he'd use for a dog, he's still the police.

I think.

"You received your summons, yes?" Thorn asks, his emerald green eyes narrowing as he waits for an answer. God, why is he looking at me like that? His eyes are so gorgeous I want to memorize them, but I don't want to stare quite as obviously as he is.

"Yes, but I can't go," I say, raising my chin.

"That's not your decision to make," Rocco says. "Or your boss's. You were summoned by the Society of Supernaturals. You're going."

"I have to work." Even though I really want to go, saying no is my only option. If I don't fight this, Silas will definitely take it out on me later, or worse, my dad. Plus, these guys just barging in and bossing me around makes me less than thrilled to go anywhere with them. They may be freakishly gorgeous, but their manners leave something to be desired.

Silas looks at me with a strange expression before turning to the two hotties I can't stop staring at. "She's my servant. If she wants to stay, I grant her that right."

"The law says even slaves have to go to the Unleashing ceremony."

"Slave?" I demand. What the hell? I'm no one's slave. Silas might own my working hours, but no one owns *me*.

"She's headstrong," Silas says, splaying his hand toward me as if to demonstrate. "I told her to go, but she refused."

My jaw drops.

"You liar," I blurt out, unable to hold my tongue any longer. I may be a lowly servant who barely earns enough to pay for bread, but I still have a spine. "I showed you my invitation, and you ripped it into pieces."

Rocco turns to Silas and gives him a look I would hate to be the one receiving. Silas shrinks visibly, and I almost feel sorry for the bastard.

"Everyone must go," Thorn says, his voice as icy as his gaze. "Now take off those gloves and come, or we'll be late for the Unleashing."

Chapter 2

Priceless is the only way to describe the look on Silas's face as Thorn and Rocco drag me out the back door.

I wish I had that effect on him. Although I'm secretly reveling in it, I know there'll be hell to pay later, so I do the only thing I can think to soften the blow. "I'll make up my hours later, Silas," I call. "I promise."

"All right, Cinderella," Rocco says with a smirk that makes a dimple appear in his cheek, too. "Let's go. As much as I enjoyed seeing you on your knees, we've got places to be."

"Well, I hope you took a mental picture of me *on my knees*," I shoot back with a sugary smile. "Because that's the last time you'll ever see it."

The smirk widens into a real smile, and he lets his eyes flick down to my breasts for just a fraction of a second. Long enough to let me know he wants to check me out, but not long enough for him to actually do the checking out. He might be tempted, but he's not going to ogle the likes of me, in my canvas overalls and work shirt.

"Too bad," he murmurs, holding my gaze for a second.

I yank my gaze from his, unnerved by this gorgeous guy who seems to be toying with me. Thorn strides ahead, crossing the parking lot toward a shiny black town car. Thankfully, the rain has stopped as they walk me to the vehicle. It's one of those super fancy ones you see in the movies. They have a driver and everything.

Thorn opens the back door and points to the seat. "Move it, girl. We're late."

It takes everything in me not to go off on the guy as I climb in and scoot to the other door. Rocco and Thorn climb in beside me, and then the car takes off through the washed out and nearly flooded streets of Jacksonville.

"You know how this works, right, Cinderella?" Rocco asks.

I offer him a glare. "Are you seriously talking to me?"

18

"Yeah, I'm talking to you," Rocco says. He grins, showing off a perfect set of glowing, white teeth.

Holding my tongue seems to be my superpower these days, especially considering how hard it is to do, but I refuse to acknowledge his insult. In answer, I turn and stare out the window, trying to memorize the route in case I need to get back home. Which at some point, I will, and I'm not trusting these assholes to return me to where they found me.

Thorn snorts with suppressed laughter.

"Hey, I think Cinderella fits," Rocco says mockingly. "Did you see her working? The girl has a talent. In fact, I've got something else she can polish…"

Did I say holding my tongue was a superpower? Scratch that.

Turning back, I glare at Rocco, determined not to let his drool-worthy jawline and bright blue eyes deter me.

"You're awfully brave, taunting a salty teenager with untested magic. Keep it up, and I just may turn your dick into an earthworm. You know. *By accident.*"

Rocco licks his lips. "I like my women salty."

"I'm not your woman," I say with a glare. "Why don't you crawl back into your cave, Neanderthal?"

Rocco starts to speak again, but Thorn cuts in. "You know what to expect at the Unleashing?"

Peeling my death stare from Rocco, I turn to Thorn. "Sure. Everyone with magical heritage is called to the Unleashing Ceremony at age eighteen, and if we have magic, it's unlocked by the highest sorcerers."

"Do you know why we wait until you're eighteen?"

"Everyone knows that."

He raises his eyebrows as if sending me a message to grow up. "Magic is mature then, and hopefully, so is the one who wields it."

"I've been working full time for the last two years. Don't worry. I'm mature enough to wield magic responsibly." Then, because I can't help myself, I add, "I won't turn any dicks into earthworms unless I'm absolutely sure they deserve it."

"Those of us with the most powerful magic will unleash everyone else's powers. If you have significant magic, you'll go to the Academy of Sorcery to master your gifts."

"You realize Silas will never go for that," I say. "Even if I do have magic, he'd never let me out of my contract. The guy hates my family with a passion."

"Silas will just have to deal," Rocco says. "Everyone with powerful magic goes to the Academy. Period."

I like the way this guy thinks. And looks.

Thorn raises an eyebrow. "Unless you're just a psychic like your mother," he says. "You can take online classes for that scant amount of magic."

Just when I thought they might not be completely insufferable.

"I'm aware," I say, giving him my frostiest smile. "I'm more interested in this Academy you mentioned."

"Even descendants of magic often don't inherit," Rocco says. "Those who do are sorted into houses for light and dark magic."

"Light and dark? Like, good and bad?"

That's something I've never heard before. Since Mom didn't go to any academy, I don't know much about it. I assume her magic was light, since her psychic gifts were low-key. Silas? Dark all the way.

"Light magic generally includes wizards, some witches, casters, magicians and such. Then dark magic includes warlocks, other witches, enchantresses, and sorcerers."

21

"What are you?"

"Higher up on the food chain than a psychic," Thorn says with a frown.

I grit my teeth and ignore that little dig at my humble magical origins. "Does that mean dark magic wielders are evil people?"

Rocco throws back his head and lets out a belly laugh. Not even five minutes with these guys, and I already know Rocco is gonna drive me to drink. Reviving my death glare, I give him a one-word reminder. "Earthworm."

Another chuckle erupts, this time from them both.

"Your mother was a psychic," Rocco says, still grinning. "Not powerful enough to even break the skin, much less do anything else to us."

"We'll see," I say lightly.

"Do you have any clue who you're messing with, Cinderella?" Rocco asks.

Maybe this banter is a game for him. Fine by me. Two can play that game. You don't live in the bad part of Jacksonville after twenty years of natural disasters uprooted the city and brought supernaturals into the light without learning how to deflect unwanted attention.

I'm no damn doormat.

"Do you have any idea who *you're* messing with?" My narrowed gaze shoots daggers at him. "In case you hadn't read my file thoroughly enough, my mother killed Silas's wife. Clearly she was powerful enough to break the skin. And if my powers are anywhere near as fatal as hers, you may regret getting on my bad side later."

"Magical inheritance is a game of chance," Thorn interjects. "It often skips a generation. IE, *you*."

"Yeah," Rocco says, crossing his muscular arms and giving me a gloating grin. "So, I wouldn't be so cocky just yet. Right now, you're nothing more than Silas's *servant*."

"Well, I guess we'll just have to see how *not powerful* I am when my magic is unleashed."

"If," Thorn corrects.

"Fine," I say, tossing my blonde hair back. "But where do you get off calling me girl? What are you, twenty?"

Rocco gives another little snort of suppressed laughter. Obviously, he likes it when I don't just roll over for them. The way these guys look, they're probably used to girls giving them whatever they want just for a smile. I don't really know what to make of him. Thorn seems to defend me one second and join Rocco in his taunting the next.

This *is* kind of fun, though, I have to admit.

Being employed by Silas doesn't exactly give me a lot of time to go out and party like other people my age. I try to accept it because that's just the way it is, but if I'm being honest, my life kinda sucks. Even if I don't have a lick of magic, at least I have this one morning to flirt with The Buff and The Beautiful. I may as well make the most of it. It sure as hell beats scrubbing toilets.

In fact, it's shaping up to be a nice break from work either way. The sun is trying to peek out from behind the clouds, and the city has a nice clean look after the night's rain. Ten minutes later, the car stops behind a really cool looking building with a sign over its doors, something in Latin I obviously can't read.

My jaw nearly drops as I get out of the town car and glance around at the Academy of Sorcery, which I've heard of even though I've never been here. The campus is a sprawling old timey estate with some outlying buildings surrounding one main building that looks like Dracula's castle. The front building even has one of those tall, skinny bell towers at the top.

Around it, a bunch of other buildings stand facing a quad of flowers and other pretty shrubbery. The campus is small but looks like it can house a decent number of students.

"So, this is where the Unleashing happens?" I ask. "On the campus itself?"

"Yes," Thorn says. "Let's go, girl."

"How many students actually go here?" I ask. "Are they just from Florida? The greater Jacksonville area?"

Hand over my eyes to shield them from the sun, I stare at the archaic but beautiful architecture as we make our way up a concrete walkway. The building's made of huge, pretty stones. Mostly gray, though some have different hues of other natural colors.

God, what I wouldn't give to go here. But I know that even if I have more magic than Mom, enough to go here, it won't void my contract. Silas can probably claim he'll teach me himself, and then he'll siphon off my magic to use for himself. The bastard.

With his hand on my upper back, Rocco leads me toward a walkway stretching toward a large building with a domed roof set back from the towering spires of the front building.

"Here we are, Cinderella. The Great Hall." Rocco laughs as he pushes open the door to a huge auditorium full of a few hundred people. "Your last hour of freedom before you get sent back to the salt mines."

"Is your family in there?" Thorn asks.

I shake my head, not wanting to go into detail about my family. They probably already know too much about my mother, and I'm not in a hurry to share personal details about my dad.

With his hand on the middle of my back now, Rocco guides me to a door off the side, which leads into a huge room where several dozen people my age are dressing and primping in front of mirrors. The moment we step inside, all eyes turn our way. I catch more than a few hungry glances fixing on my escorts.

Rocco snaps his fingers at a group of three girls, and they all scamper over like eager puppies.

"Jade, Bella," Thorn says. "Bella, Jade. Can you make sure she finds some suitable attire?"

He gestures lazily at the trio, so I can't tell which one is Bella. They all size me up like I'm a lioness approaching their fresh kill and they're not sure they want to share.

"Keep an eye on this one." Rocco points at me. "She'll probably try to bolt."

"I hope she's running to the store to buy something decent to wear to the ceremony," says the blonde in the group. "The clothes here are so off-the-rack."

"Is that a *she?*" asks one of the others, an Asian girl with pin-straight black hair styled in an asymmetrical cut that perfectly highlights her cheekbones and full lips.

The third girl in the group has light brown hair with highlights, but she's probably the type that calls that *bronde* and her shoulder length cut a *lob*.

"Hard to tell," says the blonde. "I actually thought it was a troll, not a human." Magic School Barbie is wearing a flowing silk gown, which looks every bit as perfect as her sleek platinum hair, flawless make-up, and glimmering straight teeth.

In contrast, I'm still wearing my work clothes, with my hair in a sloppy bun I threw in after getting drenched this morning, and I smell faintly of disinfectant. Luckily, Blonde Bella seems to have momentarily forgotten me as she smiles adoringly up at Thorn, fluttering her eyelashes.

Thorn doesn't seem to notice. He reads something on his phone, shows it to Rocco, and they step aside to confer in the corner.

Brunette Bella's brown eyes widen as she looks me over, and she holds in a laugh, covering her mouth with her perfectly manicured nails. You know, the long pointy ones that could put an eye out in one vicious swipe. "Where did you even get those clothes? Out of a Dumpster?"

I roll my eyes and cross my arms over my chest. "I realize I don't look like I'm going to the ball today, but in my defense, I was at work when these guys dragged me here."

I was expecting to be cleaning toilets all day, not standing in front of the entire magical community of Florida, but I decide not to make matters worse by mentioning the toilets to a Bella.

Not that she'd care. She's probably never cleaned a thing in her life.

"I suppose even magic schools need janitors," says the blonde. She titters, and her posse giggles along with her.

I set my hands on my hips and give her a once over. "Guess every magic school needs a bitch."

Bella's mouth drops open, but her black-haired friend steps forward. "Oh, sweetheart. You *really* don't want to mess with us."

"Oh, but sweetheart, I really do." I step even closer than she dared to get. Seems we're about the same height, so I stare her right in the eyes. Two can play this game, and I don't back down from this kind of girl. I've seen a lot worse on the streets of my neighborhood than a spoiled little princess with an attitude.

Just as Bella seems about to unleash her fury, Thorn grabs her arm, and Rocco grabs mine.

"I leave you alone for five minutes, and you're already starting trouble," Rocco growls as his huge hand grips my forearm with firm pressure.

"You don't have to watch me." I jerk away, halfway because his touch is strangely comforting, and I don't want to be calmed. "I can take care of myself, and I'm not going to run away. If I've learned anything in my life, it's that there's no escaping some things. Magic and Silas are two of them."

"And the Unleashing," Thorn says. He casts a glare at Blonde Bella, and she turns in a huff and storms away with her posse.

"Look around you, Cinderella." Rocco leans down, so close I can smell the clean, soapy smell of him, and a tang of masculine musk that intoxicates me. He taps the tip of my nose with a fingertip. "You're surrounded by power. You don't want to piss off the wrong person."

His eyes lock on mine for a beat, so close I can see the darker flecks in his marbled blue eyes. My pulse flutters, and Rocco smirks like he somehow knows. Instead of mocking me, he abruptly straightens and pushed out the door, leaving me standing alone with Thorn.

"He's right, Jade." Thorn's emerald orbs are every bit as captivating as Rocco's, but his are serious. "You don't know if you'll be attending the Academy for the next four years. You don't want to be on the wrong side of some of the families here."

Plenty of people still use magic to gain power and wealth, just as they did before 'coming out' to humans. Now they don't have to hide it, but it's not much different. I've never bought into the magic scene, though I've watched some of the reality shows—*America's Next Top Vampire, Kitty Chasers, My Fairytale Life*. It hadn't really occurred to me until this moment that some of the magic wielders in Jacksonville might be rich and famous. Magic has never been a big part of my life, even when Mom was alive. Hers was so insignificant it didn't affect our lives much, and since then, just surviving took up most of my time and attention.

As I scan the room, I notice more than a few expensive gowns. I cross my arms, feeling even more like the Ugly Duckling. "Thanks," I say quietly to Thorn. "For looking out for me."

"I wasn't," he says, his jaw set. He looks like he's about to storm out, but then he hesitates, dips his head and whispers in my ear, "Don't bite the hand that feeds you."

His mouth brushes against my ear, and warm chills rush across my skin at the contact. I shiver with anticipation, but Thorn straightens and disappears out the door without another word.

"Are the Bellas starting shit already? Figures."

My eyes snap open, and I see a tall emo guy standing in front of me. Beside him, hanging a step back, hovers a pale girl with mousy brown hair and an ill-fitting dress.

"That was impressive," he says.

I force a laugh. "Thanks."

"I'm Asher," he says. "This is Elowen."

Asher is tall, thin, and adorable in a guyliner-heavy way. Elowen is unremarkable except for a pair of huge, luminous brown eyes peering out from her pale face.

"Hi," she says with a tiny wave.

I nod at the two of them, grateful to have a couple friendly faces in this sea of strangers. "So, they're the resident mean girls here?"

"They went to our high school," Asher explains. "They made friends in, like, Kindergarten because they're all named Bella. And judging from the past hour, they've already established themselves as the Ones to Watch."

"Now that you're on her radar, you're kind of screwed," Elowen says, biting at a hangnail.

"Girl, I'm from the ghetto," I said. "People like her don't scare me."

Asher purses his lips, which are plump and pierced and possibly coated with gloss. "We're going to be friends," he says. He plants a hand on his hip and points to my outfit, scanning my body from head to toe with one finger. "But if you want to hang with us, you have got to do something about that outfit."

He's wearing a distressed grey T-shirt, ripped skinny jeans, and combat boots, and his black hair is slicked back with gel. And though he's critiquing me, I can't help but like him already. He tells it like it is, which is just my style.

"They have clothes for us," Elowen says, hooking her thumb toward some makeshift dressing rooms set up behind curtains. "Everyone who's anyone will be here to watch the Unleashing. They want us dressed to the nines."

As we go through racks of clothes, searching for the perfect dresses and a suit for Asher, they fill me in on the competition.

"Definitely steer clear of the Bellas," Asher says. "Especially Bella Goodwin—the blonde. She'll do whatever it takes to get what she wants. And trust me when I say she always gets it. Her daddy's on the board of the Society of Supernaturals itself."

"And what is it that she wants?" I ask, unimpressed.

"The one thing she knows she can't have. Thorn Cristofaro." He wiggles his pierced eyebrows at me. Obviously, I'm not the only one who thinks that jerk is mouthwatering.

"He's the only guy she couldn't get in high school," Elowen says.

"And the only guy she *didn't* get, if you know what I mean," Asher says. He holds up a skinny suit, and we both give him the thumbs up.

Elowen nudges Asher. "Except you."

"Even if the thought of eating pussy didn't make me squeamish, I wouldn't touch that snake with a ten-foot pole," Asher says. "No offense to your pussies. I'm sure they're lovely."

"My pussy takes no offense," I say, laughing. I can't believe we got here so fast.

Elowen holds up a shiny black gown against her wispy frame and gives us a questioning look, chewing at her lip. From the next row over, Blonde Bella points at us and lets out a nasty laugh. "Look, Bellas. The janitor already found some trash to take out."

Elowen shoves the dress back on the rack, her face reddening. Even though it was not the right dress for my new friend, and it might have resembled a trash bag a teensy bit, I jump to her defense. "Yeah, I found some trash," I say, pointing at Bella. "Right there. Let me show you to your Dumpster."

"Don't make me come over this rack, bitch," she says.

"Don't start what you can't finish," I say.

"Oh, I'll finish," she says. "You just wait. It's coming."

"I won't hold my breath," I say. Shaking my head, I turn back to Asher and Elowen. "You were saying?"

Asher laughs. "You're a keeper."

"So, you went to high school with those bitches, huh? My apologies."

"Where'd you go?" Asher asks, holding a rich, purple dress against my curvy frame. "I don't recognize you."

"Oh, you know," I say, trying to sound light. "I dropped out a few years ago."

I don't want to unload the whole depressing story. I'm here, on the precipice of a brand-new start. I'm going to make the best of it, dammit.

"I'm sorry," Elowen says, looking up at me with big, sad eyes. I have a feeling I'm not the only person here with a sad story.

Before I can ask if she wants to talk about it, the door swings open and another gorgeous hunk of man strides in. He's got a hard set to his chiseled jaw, and an even harder look in his eyes, but it doesn't detract from his striking masculine beauty. His blond hair is cut short on the sides and slicked back on top, and his jawline would make any man in America envious. The air in the room seems to crackle when he walks in, and my mouth literally starts to water as I take in every inch of his tall, lean, muscular build.

Where the hell do they grow these guys?

His eyes take in the room full of candidates for the Academy of Sorcery. In one glance, he dismisses all of us. "Five minutes," he says, then disappears out the door.

"Hurry," Asher says, grabbing me and Elowen and dragging us toward the dressing rooms. "The Unleashing is about to begin."

Chapter 3

Like a migration of brightly colored butterflies, we stream out into the auditorium where a platform is set up in front. There are hordes of people in the audience, proud magical parents and relatives in addition to the all-important Society of Supernatural members.

Dad is obviously not in attendance. I don't know if a fire could drag him out of the house.

Once on the platform, I half-heartedly glance out into the crowd, searching for him nonetheless. Just in case. Maybe he changed his mind about the Unleashing after all. Maybe he showed up for me.

Unsurprisingly, he's nowhere to be found. Refusing to let myself feel disappointed, I turn back to the platform above, where the magic of soothsayers and psychics, empaths and telepaths will be unleashed on the world. Well, not really on the world. That's why the Academy exists.

So yeah. I have bigger things to worry about today than whether my dad stepped out of his comfort zone to see if I am a magical legacy or not.

Up on the stage, the mean-looking hottie from the changing room starts to speak, getting my full attention.

"Welcome," he says, opening his arms. He's wearing some kind of cloak, so when he spreads his arms, the garment spreads like shimmering black wings. His voice easily carries over the whole crowd like he's speaking into an invisible, magical microphone. The murmuring crowd falls silent, the air charged with anticipation. "I'm Ryker Steele, a sorcery student at the academy. On behalf of the staff and faculty of the Academy of Sorcery and Other Magical Arts, we thank you for your attendance at this year's Unleashing Ceremony."

I notice how they just shorten it to Academy of Sorcery when not talking to the heads of the magical community, like no one else is important. After all, sorcerers are the most powerful of all, the ones capable of controlling the magic of all others—both binding it at birth and unleashing it at age eighteen. Oh, well. I won't have to deal with these snobs much longer.

Ryker goes on. "Esteemed Society of Supernatural members, Witch and Wizard Council, family, friends, and academy candidates, please enjoy this year's Unleashing. Let us begin."

To my surprise, both Rocco and Thorn appear out of thin air, one on either side of Ryker. A gasp goes up from the audience. They are similarly attired—black skinny pants, shimmering black cloaks that seem to drip with magic somehow, as black as the night sky and shimmering as if they contain the universe of stars.

Beside me, Asher gives a breathy sigh.

I knew these guys had something to do with this, but finding out they're actually two of the four who unleash powers makes me a little nauseous.

Thorn's warning makes a lot more sense now. There I was smarting off to them like a brat, and they're not just hired goons for the academy, out to chase down errant magical progeny. They're freaking *sorcerers*.

"Good morning," says the fourth man to appear on the platform. He takes the steps up, skipping the fanfare. He addresses the group of recruits instead of the crowd filling the seats.

"I'm Professor Darius, Head Sorcerer and instructor here at the academy," he says. Somewhere around six feet, he's got chestnut brown hair, chiseled features, and chocolate brown eyes. Everything from his neatly cut and styled hair, to his entrance, to the way he addresses the prospective students in a kind manner that settles my nerves tells me he's nothing like the other three sorcerers. Not to mention he's tall and lean, while they look like they were transported from a body building magazine. He looks classy. They're almost thuggish.

"I'm going to faint," Asher whispers, fanning himself. "He's even more gorgeous in person than online."

"Deep breaths," I whisper, trying not to laugh at his reaction.

Professor Darius glances at us, and I could swear he heard us, the way his eyes linger just a second too long. Heat shimmers along my limbs. Damn. Now I need to be fanned. He takes 'hot for teacher' to a whole new level.

Term 1: Unleashing Trials

"As is known, the four most powerful wielders of magic are responsible for releasing the magic within the new recruits," the professor says. He goes on for a minute while I ogle the sorcerers. Maybe hotness is a requirement for being a sorcerer. Or maybe their high magic level makes them somehow irresistible to lowly minions like me. All of them could incite butterfly riots.

More than that, they're fucking powerful. Four masters of all magic. I didn't let them intimidate me before, but considering what they're capable of, I probably shouldn't have let my smart mouth get so out of hand. Standing here with the nervously shifting new recruits, it finally feels real. These guys are no joke. This ceremony isn't only going to tell me if I'm blessed with magic. It will affect the rest of my life.

Before I can bring my train of thought back to the little speech the professor is giving, it's over, and the first recruit is walking up the stairs to the stage, her legs visibly quaking.

My mind wanders again. Why did two advanced students from the academy come looking for me? I'd think a servant girl working for a warlock would be small potatoes to ranked sorcerers like them.

"Kneel," Professor Darius says in a commanding but gentle tone.

The girl does as she's told, gets down on her knees, closes her eyes, and waits. Even from here, I can see her hyperventilating, though I can't tell if it's nervousness or excitement.

The four sorcerers lay their hands on her head while Professor Darius sets his fingers on the center of her forehead and closes his eyes.

"Deep within our souls we hold and hide the power of the universe until such time as it's ready to blossom," Darius says. "From the core of your being, from the point of all creation, we four ambassadors of magic unleash and unlock your power."

For a second, it looks like nothing's going to happen.

Until it does.

"Unleash," the four sorcerers say as one.

The girl starts trembling again, only this time it's so forceful that I'm a little scared for her. A strange blue light emanates from her and bursts through the room, and then it's gone.

"House of light witches," the professor declares.

Term 1: Unleashing Trials

A round of applause fills the arena, and the smile on the girl's face is infectious. Apparently, she's stoked with her magical designation.

"This is kind of cool," I whisper to my new friends.

After the first girl, Professor Darius calls name after name, unlocking magic within those who have it and dismissing those who don't. The myriad of emotional energy pouring through the arena right now is palpable. Whether magical or not, everybody seems to have an opinion. Disappointment exudes from those who have no magic, while anxiety and excitement come from those who do.

Finally Elowen is called. She wobbles up the steps, even paler than before. She stands before the four sorcerers for a second and then drops to her knees like it's the only thing saving her from fainting dead away. I find myself squeezing my hands into fists, rooting for her to get something good as the sorcerers place their hands on her head. Professor Darius touches her forehead, then says the incantation. After a moment, black wisps of something that looks like smoke begin to rise from her head. The three younger sorcerers draw back a bit, looking tense, as if they expect frail little Elowen to bite them.

This hasn't happened to anyone yet. I glance at Asher, who looks as startled as I feel.

"House of Necromancy," Professor Darius says.

Elowen's eyes burst open, and her jaw drops. "No, it can't be true," she cries in a desperate voice. She glances up to the professor as if imploring him to change his mind. "I'm not evil," she says, her voice shaking. "I can't be evil." She reaches out and grabs the professor's wrists. "Please. Pick something else."

"I didn't choose Necromancy," he says gently. "It chose you. Dark magic is dark, not evil."

The professor reaches down to help Elowen up, but she flops onto the stage and starts to sob uncontrollably. I can't help but feel sorry for her. I wouldn't want to have magic that could raise the dead, either. A second later, an old grisly dude dressed in black robes appears on the back of the stage, grabs Elowen by the arm, pulls her to her feet, and drags her off the platform.

"What the hell?" I bark, angered by the way they just treated her, no matter what magic she has. The three sorcery students stood there looking at her like she carried plague.

Ryker shakes his head as the man in black disappears with my new acquaintance. He looks on with his lip curled in disgust. "Drama queens. Always have to make a scene."

Just when I thought I might be able to tolerate one of the guys, he blows it. He's as much of a dickbag as Rocco. I seriously hope I don't have any classes with these assholes.

After a few more non-magical progenies walk out, disappointed to be normal, it's Asher's turn. He rushes up the steps and gets to his knees. After the ceremonial words, Professor Darius announces that Asher is a wizard. Asher grins as he gets to his feet and walks off to join his new comrades who will be joining the House of Wizardry.

Waiting nervously, I stand in line a few more minutes until it's my turn. Though I'm so excited and nervous that my stomach churns, my knees are strong as I climb onto the stage.

Magic is passed down through DNA, so there's a fifty-fifty shot that I could have some. Unless Thorn is right, and it skips a generation. That would suck. If I get my mom's power, no doubt I'll be a little disappointed, but at least I won't have to walk out with my head hung in shame. Not that being psychic is anything to write home about. I'll take a few online classes and maybe earn some money reading fortunes on the side while working for Silas for the next bazillion years. At least I'll know when to leave early because of flooding.

"Took your sweet time getting up here," Rocco grumbles.

I roll my eyes at him.

Ryker points to the floor. "Knees."

Rocco leans in and whispers into my ear. "You're used to being on your knees, right, Cinderella?"

I turn my face up to him and give him my most charming smile. "Earthworm," I whisper, crooking my little finger at him.

"Not here," Ryker snaps at Rocco before he can say whatever pervy thing was coming to his dirty mind.

"She does have a strong sexual energy," the professor says quietly, so only the four of us can hear.

"Seriously?" Humiliated, I hiss out my words, not caring that he might be my teacher soon. "What the hell does that mean?"

"It's nothing to be ashamed of," Darius says. "Please kneel as we unleash your power."

Term 1: Unleashing Trials

Letting out a sigh, I get down to my knees, hoping to get out of this without losing whatever dignity I have left.

Eyes closed, I try to relax and ignore a fuss that's going on in the crowd below while the four sorcerers put their hands on my head. With bated breath, I wait as the four sorcerers say, "Unleash."

At the same moment, someone below the platform yells, "Stop!"

But it's too late. A strange, searing heat rushes through my veins, getting stronger until it's crushing into my chest and exploding from inside me. Hot light flashes behind my eyelids, and my entire body—like, every nerve and muscle— explodes with some kind of ancient, primal energy I can't even describe in words. I gasp, falling back from their hands.

Heat is pulsing so hard between my legs I can't tell if I want to scream with pleasure or pain. A need is ripping apart my insides, like the entire universe depends on if I satisfy this craving right this very instant. I curl onto my side, biting down on my fingertips so I won't plunge them between my aching thighs. I force my eyes open, realizing that I'm lying on the stage floor. But no one is staring and laughing.

Three men in black-trimmed purple robes are on the stage, holding back the sorcery students, who are looking at me with a kind of smoldering lust that makes my need pulse even stronger. I gasp in pain, biting down on my lip as my hands slide down my body, caressing my curves. Rocco's mouth is literally hanging open, and Thorn's eyes are locked on mine with such force I almost cry out. Ryker's eyes are squeezed shut, but I can see a pronounced ridge straining at his slacks. I gulp, my clit throbbing with the beginning of something I definitely don't want to happen in an arena full of spectators.

A man with short white whiskers and a Santa belly is red-faced and yelling at Professor Darius, and beyond them…

I swallow hard, caught between lust and horror as I see the crowd in the arena. It seems I'm not the only one caught in this madness. People are tearing off their own clothes and the clothes of those next to them. Couples are kissing, groups are groping, and I spot one naked woman riding a man for all she's worth while a man behind her is groping her breasts, his eyes rolling back in his head in pure bliss. As I tear my eyes away, I only find more of the same.

Kissing. Rubbing. Blowjobs. Dudes going down on women. Or other dudes. Girl on girl, guy on guy, nobody seems to care who they're with as long as they have someone to bang.

Holy. Fucking. Shit.

This cannot be real. It feels like I'm dreaming, though I know I'm not.

What the hell is happening? And better yet, why?

Professor Darius did say something about my sexual energy beforehand. Did I do this? No way. It can't be. But oh my god, I want him. Or any of them. My body is on fire, like I'm filled with lava. I crawl toward Ryker, who's closest to me. I grab his legs and climb him like a monkey, running my lips along the ridge in his pants. He lets out a loud hiccupping sound as the guy holding him tries to push me away. But there's nothing that can stop me now. I throw myself into his arms, wrapping my legs around him. The second our bodies collide, pleasure like nothing I've ever felt wracks my body, and I bite back a cry, shuddering against him as my entire body pulses again and again.

A second later, Darius grabs me from behind and drags me off. I don't care who's touching me, I just have to be touched.

I turn and throw my arms around Darius, and he hurries me through a curtain and off the back of the stage, where the old dude took Elowen. The herd of magical people follow, and I feel something pressing back the magic, subduing me and returning me to my senses. The guy who was yelling at Professor Darius is performing some kind of chant that I can only hope is a sex magic exorcism, because this cannot go on. I just humped a guy until I orgasmed in front of the entire magical community, for fuck's sake.

And if Professor Darius doesn't put me down, I'm about to do it again.

Chapter 4

"What the hell was that?" I demand as I detach myself from Professor Darius in a small office now crowded with the three sorcery students, their professor, and two purple-robed guys. I'd be more embarrassed if I wasn't so pissed, so I try to hold onto the anger. If I have to choose between the two, I'll choose pissed any day.

Whatever magic happened, it seems to have released me from its hold, but there's no way I'm looking at Ryker or Professor Darius right now. Or the two assholes who dragged me out of Silas's basement. For all I know, they knew I'd go sex crazy when I got unleashed.

Since I can't look at anyone from the academy, I focus on the flustered-looking Santa guy instead, trying to ignore the distant sounds of the madness still happening out in the arena.

"Seriously, dude. What. Was. That?"

"I've never seen anything like it," Professor Darius admits as he sits in a chair against the wall. His forehead is glistening with sweat. "You can relax, you're safe now."

"Safe?" Rocco asks, looking like he's about to pounce on his professor and strangle him. "What the fuck did she do to us?"

"Well, we know what she did to Ryker," Thorn mutters, glaring at me like I personally insulted him.

Ryker stares stone-faced at the Santa guy. "What is she?" he asks flatly.

Seeing him beside Rocco, the same shade of blond hair and same wide, blue eyes, it's clear they're related. Rocco is more muscular, barrel chested like a strongman, while Ryker is leaner and taller, but their facial features leave no doubt. Great. Two asshole brothers. Just what every girl needs.

"Who retrieved this student?" the Santa guy asks. "Didn't you read her summons letter?"

"She didn't have one," Thorn growls, still glaring daggers at me.

"Said she flushed it down the toilet," Rocco says with a smirk at me, clearly hoping this will get him off the hook. He crosses his arms over his massive chest and puffs it out, an alpha-hole move he probably uses to intimidate people. Well fuck that.

I didn't choose whatever the fuck just happened, and I sure as hell won't back down and take this shit. "My employer tore it up," I say coldly. "And can someone please fill me in on what the hell just happened?"

"We'd like an explanation as well," Ryker says through clenched teeth, keeping his gaze trained on the older man instead of looking at me.

"You're the ones who unleashed my magic," I snap, since I do not appreciate people talking about me like I'm not here. "Shouldn't you have known that would happen?"

"Everyone, just calm down." Professor Darius is back up on his feet and looking a little more normal and less flushed. "Unfortunately, Master Hardin, we didn't have her letter, so we didn't know this was one of the students you had identified as a potential carrier. We had no way of knowing that would happen."

"It should have been in the registry," the man splutters to another one of the purple-robed guys. "What did I tell you? There was bound to be a mistake."

"Seriously, guys," I said. "Total newbie right here. What the what?"

"I'm sorry," the old guy says, holding out a hand. "I'm Master Hardin, the senior sorcerer in the Society of Supernaturals. I represent the magic wielders in the Society. I'm also the head of affairs for such people as ourselves."

Well, isn't this super? I just dry-humped a sorcerer in front of the magical equivalent of the president.

"Jade," I say, shaking his hand because what else can I do?

His grip is firm and grounding, his eyes kind. "I know."

"I'm Headmaster Orville," says one of the other purple-robed men. He's way older than Master Hardin, bent and twisted like an ancient oak, with a bald head and round glasses. "The headmaster of this Academy and also a member of the Society of Supernaturals."

Term 1: Unleashing Trials

Master Hardin begins to explain. "When your magic was bound at birth, you were marked as someone who had the potential for… Extraordinary magic. That's why these powerful men were sent to get you when you were late to arrive. Unfortunately, giving them details could have endangered you if they ran into any telepaths or interested parties on their way, so they weren't informed of your potential."

"But they were instructed to retrieve you and make sure you made it safely to the Unleashing," the headmaster says.

"Uh huh," I say, nodding like a bobble head. That explains why they showed up to get me, and why they told someone to keep an eye on me while I was getting dressed. But I still don't get what just happened.

"I've never seen this before, but from what we experienced today, I believe that you are the next High Priestess."

"The what now?" I ask. I'm pretty sure I've heard of all the magical people from conjurers to illusionists, enchantresses and empaths, but I've never heard of any priestess who causes spontaneous orgies.

"That's not possible," Thorn says in a low voice. He's staring at me like I've grown tentacles out of my ass.

The other two sorcerers are eyeing me warily, too. Even Rocco's smart-ass smirk is gone. Ryker's finally looking at me instead of through me, but he looks like he's about to bolt out the door if I make a sudden movement. If I thought he gave Elowen the evil eye for making a scene, I should have waited for the looks they're giving me.

Professor Darius clears his throat. "Master, if I may," he says. "Has something happened to the High Priestess? We've always been told there's only one, and surely we would have heard if something had happened to the current High Priestess."

"The real one," Thorn growls, glaring at me like I killed this lady I've never heard of so I can take her place.

"As you are aware, the current High Priestess is a member of the undead," Headmaster Orville points out. "We anticipated that this day could come. We simply didn't know where or if she'd really appear."

"I see," Ryker says, nodding. I can see a light dawning in all their eyes, but I still have no fucking clue what's happening.

"Somebody care to explain what the hell is going on?" I ask.

"The undead have died at some point," Thorn points out.

"I am aware," I grit out, leveling him with a glare.

"When one High Priestess dies, another is instantly granted powers," Master Hardin explains. "It can be anyone of any age in the world, as long as they possess the potential to wield great magic. Someone such as yourself, Jade."

"So I won the sex-magic lottery?" I ask, trying to make light of it. "Lucky me."

"It's usually a descendant, but in some instances, the High Priestess hasn't had children, or her children don't hold the potential. Then someone is gifted the magic at random, yes. What makes this case unique is that the High Priestess didn't stay dead. So, now we have two."

"Which is a good thing," Professor Darius says, though he doesn't look all that excited if you ask me. "Jade will have time to train and prepare, control her magic, and practice wielding it safely."

"Yes," Master Hardin says. "Sometimes, the recipient of the gift is not so fortunate, and she learns the hard way what her magic is capable of."

"Okay," I say. "Cool, cool. But how come I've never heard of this person? What's so important about her?"

The men exchange a look. Master Hardin speaks again, his voice soothing. "The High Priestess is the embodiment of the divine feminine. She bore many names throughout history, perhaps most famously Aphrodite."

"Wait, what?" I asked, backing into the wall. I think I'm going to have a heart attack. "I'm...a goddess?"

"Call it what you like," Master Hardin says. "High Priestess is our preferred term."

"What does that mean for us?" Rocco demands. "For the Academy?"

"The High Priestess is the source of all sexual energy," Master Hardin says. "It will be difficult for Jade to be around men until her magic is harnessed—both for her and the men she encounters. It is of utmost importance that she find a magical vessel to contain some of her energy while she trains."

"Of course," Professor Darius says, giving a small nod.

"Are you sure you didn't identify her incorrectly?" Ryker asks, giving me some serious stink-eye. I give him a pass this time, considering how gross I acted. Not that it's my fault, but still. He has a right to think I'm gropy and desperate. I'll just have to show him I'm not some horndog maniac who's going to rub her junk all over him without invitation.

"You witnessed the Unleashing," Master Hardin says gently to the other sorcerers. "You felt it. There is no other explanation." He fixes me a look of reverence. "She's the High Priestess."

"What exactly is going to happen now?" I ask. "People around me will want to have sex? With each other *and* me?" I stare at the professor, thinking I might not mind jumping his bones. He's sexy in that suave, hot-for-teacher kind of way, but there's something more about him. He's looking at me with a compassion I sure don't see in the three sorcery students.

"You will remain at the Academy until you've learned to harness and wield your magic," Professor Darius says. "Just like every student here."

"Am I gonna fall for every guy or girl I see?" I ask. Maybe I'm only lusting after him because of the magic.

"Since there's only one of these beings in the world, we don't have experience teaching magic to your kind," Professor Darius explains. "You will have to bear with us while we all learn together. First year students learn basic magic, which you have in spades, and to control their gift. You'll have your hands full with that."

"We will have you join in with another school of magic for the time being," Headmaster Orville says. "Until we can locate a tutor for your unique situation."

He looks to Master Hardin, who nods solemnly. "That is the best we can do for now, Jade."

"Second year students begin to focus on their unique gifts and learn more advanced magic," Professor Darius says. "That's when it will be imperative that you have a teacher who understands your situation. But don't worry. That's a year away, and we've got plenty to work on until then."

My life just got a hundred times more bizarre than it already was. Though I hoped for magic, I couldn't in my wildest dreams have predicted this.

"What about Silas?" I ask. "My boss won't be happy about this."

I'm genuinely a little freaked out. What if my magic does draw me to other people? Or them to me? That scene out there was freaky as fuck, and I definitely don't want a repeat of my sex puppet routine. Will that happen everywhere I go? What if I can't control it?

"Silas will obey the law," Master Hardin says. "You must be trained."

"As far as the law's concerned, he owns the next thirty-odd years of my life," I remind them.

"I will handle Silas and the courts. This takes precedence."

"You don't get it. I have to go back," I say, my voice rising with desperation. "They'll hurt my father."

"No work today," Headmaster Orville insists then he looks at the other men. "I am assigning these three sorcery students to protect you."

My mouth drops open. No. No fucking way.

Thorn must share my sentiments, because he begins to protest. Headmaster Orville holds up a hand to silence him. "Jade must be escorted everywhere. You can trade shifts, so you have time for your own studies and leisure activities. But I will not have the High Priestess harmed under my watch."

"You've got to be kidding me." Rocco glares at me, then back to the headmaster. "I didn't sign up for daycare duty."

"He's right," Ryker agrees. "We're students, not babysitters. Can't you find some underling to do it?"

"Her magic is too strong. She needs someone to protect her from the lure she has on others. She cannot do this alone. You must help her. It is a great honor."

"Thank you," Ryker grits out, sounding anything but honored.

The headmaster looks at the professor next. "I leave the day-to-day oversight of this matter in your hands. Her protection is paramount, Professor. Please see to it that she's taken care of."

"Wait, I still don't understand," I say. "Are you saying everywhere I go, orgies will ensue? Like, sex everywhere? Horny people gone wild, everybody banging everyone?"

Master Hardin chuckles. At least this guy has a sense of humor. I wish he were sticking around the academy. Or being my bodyguard. I'd way rather hang out with gramps here than these arrogant jerks.

"That was an effect of your magic being unleashed," he explains. "After that burst of energy, your levels will be low for a time, so you should be relatively safe for the next week or so. But men and women will still be drawn to you, and you'll be drawn to them. Even more so once your magic begins to recharge."

"Don't worry, we'll find the vessel to hold your magic soon," Professor Darius says. He reaches out and pats my arm, and a rush of tingling shimmies up my skin. The teacher draws back and smooths his hand over the lower half of his face, staring at me like I'm dangerous.

But right now, the only danger I'm worried about is Silas. More than anything, I'm worried what this means for my dad. As much as I'd like to trust that these guys can handle my boss, I can't count on that. Knowing Silas, he'll happily agree to whatever they want, then come back and take it out on me tenfold. The last time I pissed off my boss, I regretted it, and nothing has changed as far as he's concerned. He still owns my contract. Maybe I can just take night classes after work each day...

Headmaster Orville reaches out and gives my hand a quick pump. "Welcome to the Academy of Sorcery. It is a privilege to have the honor and responsibility of your education."

"Um, thanks?" I say. "I mean, thanks for accepting me. I can't wait to get started." My excitement about having magic has dimmed a bit since I learned I have weird sex magic, but I'm excited to learn basic magic with the other students, even if I have to do it around my work schedule.

The headmaster looks at the guys then. "Once her magic is contained in its vessel, Jade may return home to retrieve her things. You should escort her on this venture, of course."

For a second, I entertain the fantasy that I'll be a normal magic student. I'll put my magic in this cup or whatever, take classes with other people like me, and hang out with friends. But as much as I'd love to believe life could be that simple, I can't afford to.

My dad is too important. I can't just leave him until they find the place to store my magic. He'll be expecting me home soon, and if I don't show up, he'll… I don't know what. He's already lost everything. I can't leave him, too. Not like this. I just need a chance to tell him about the magic, and that I have to stay on campus for a few days until it's stored in its vessel. If I just disappear? I can't bear to think of him in that much pain, let alone cause it.

While the asshole twins argue over who has to take the first shift, I'm already strategizing my escape. They said I was safe for a week or so until my magic built up again, and I paid attention on the ride over. If something happens, so what? I can deal with it. I grew up on the streets of Jacksonville, dammit. This High Priestess can protect herself.

Chapter 5

After giving the guys the slip—living on the streets of Jacksonville in this day and age, it's not the first time I've had to make a quick getaway—and hotwiring the academy's town car, I use the GPS to make my way back to Silas's estate and sneak in the back door. I would go home first, but that's the first place Silas will go when I don't show up. He knows not only where I live, but where my heart lives. I won't have my father pay for my missed day of work.

Robert is setting the table for Silas's lunch when I arrive. He looks up with a curious gaze. "What happened at the Unleashing?"

"Oh, you know. Magical people got their magical gifts." I give a dismissive wave as if nothing out of the ordinary happened and open the cleaning supply closet and get my basket of stuff.

"I gather you have no magic?"

Avoiding his question because I really hate lying to people I like, I shrug it off and close the closet door. "Where's Silas?"

"In his study. You should probably know that he went to the Unleashing. He returned just a short while ago. So, if you're planning to hide anything from him, you might reconsider."

Shit. I wasn't expecting that. I wonder if he was there for the orgy. Or better yet, who he tried to bang while he was there.

Actually, scratch that. I definitely don't want to know.

"I'll just steer clear of him and do my work."

"Wise choice," the vampire says, turning back to face the stove and resuming his task of feeding the beast that is my boss.

Armed with my cleaning supplies, I sneak back down the stairs and return to the bathroom I was cleaning earlier. After a short wipe-down, I come out to find Silas standing there staring at me.

His eyes look... different. Like he's actually interested in me for reasons other than lording his position over me and making my life miserable. I never thought I'd miss the Silas of lording and life-misery making, but the change is a disturbingly unwelcome one.

"What are you doing here?" he demands.

"Um… working?" I respond. "What else would I be doing?"

Rather than saying anything, he simply stares at me.

"I'm just going to clean the rest of the bathrooms," I say, gloves on and basket of supplies in hand. I start to edge past him.

Silas says nothing. Given the creeper vibes I'm getting from him, he doesn't have to speak for me to know what he's thinking.

Maybe coming back here wasn't such a good idea after all.

For the next couple of hours, I move from one bathroom to another. All the while, Silas lurks in the shadows somewhere close enough for me to feel his icky vibe but not close enough for me to see him when I look up from my task. Occasionally, he peeks his head inside, stares at me with greedy eyes, and asks how it's coming along. The job always sucks, but now it's downright unbearable.

Finally, ten o'clock rolls around, and I've made up for my missed hours. As I put my cleaning basket back in the closet and close the door, Silas is standing in the doorway that leads out of the kitchen into his dining room.

"I'm going home now," I announce to him and Robert as I grab my raincoat off the hook and sling it over my arm. No need to put it on now. The rain stopped hours ago, and it's muggy as always outside. Silas gives me a calculating look, but then he nods that I'm released from my duties for the day. As I step out the back door, I've never been so happy in all my life to be out of that man's sight.

"You really aren't very bright, are you?" A voice says from behind me, reminding me of how I got here in the first place. Turning around, I'm faced with my clunky sedan, the shiny town car I stole, and three very unhappy sorcerers.

"What the hell were you thinking?" Thorn demands as he, Rocco, and Ryker stand in front of me.

"Nothing," Ryker says shaking his head, arms crossed over his muscular chest. "If she's even capable of thought."

"Dumb blonde," Rocco says, tugging my hair like a five-year-old.

I slap his hand away. "There's only one situation that calls for hair-pulling, and this isn't it."

"Damn," Rocco says, licking his lips. And even though he's being an ass, I can't help but stare as his tongue glides along his full, gorgeous lip.

"Professor Darius is fuming over this," Thorn says, grabbing my arm. "And nice stunt with the car. You're racking up points already. Keep this up, and you'll be expelled before the year starts."

As they haul me toward the town car, a beautiful raven-haired women suddenly appears out of thin air, blocking our way. Before I can blink, Ryker has leapt between us and holds up a hand, and a sword materializes in his grip. Impressive as fuck, I have to admit.

"Stand down," he commands.

"Jade." The woman's full, red lips curve into a smile. She appears completely unfazed by the weapon. "Finally we meet."

"What do you want?" Ryker barks.

"Well, hello boys." She smirks at Ryker, then turns her gaze to Thorn and then Rocco. Thorn drops my arm, and Rocco stares at her, transfixed.

The woman's gaze fixes on me next, and a strange tingling starts at the base of my skull and works its way down my spine.

My muscles instantly relax. "You don't really want to go to the academy, do you?" she croons.

I want to speak, but I'm as mesmerized as the rest of them.

"You have a choice. Go with them, or do magic for me. I will buy your contract from that mongrel you serve, and you'll never have to work for him again."

Freedom. The one thing I've dreamed of, the thing I never thought I'd have.

"Really?" I manage. "How?"

"Simple. I have the means to procure your contract from your slave master. You can use your magic for great things in this world, or you can scrub floors for the rest of your life. It's your choice, child."

I know something too good to be true when I hear it. "Who are you?" I ask. "And if you're buying my contract, does that mean I'm bound to you instead?"

Although I don't know this woman from Adam, I have to admit, I'm intrigued. More than that. I'm tempted. My contract with Silas is something that even the academy can't take away. Could I be free, no longer a servant to Silas? Or would I be trading one master for another?

"Jade, don't trust her," Thorn says, moving in front of me like he's trying to protect me.

Ryker shakes his head as if clearing his thoughts. He points his sword at the woman's beautiful face again. "This woman is using dark magic," he accuses. "She'll use you for evil, Jade. Don't listen to her."

"Don't you use dark magic?" I ask, remembering the explanation Thorn gave me this morning. Sorcerers fell into the dark magic category.

Before he can answer, the woman sidesteps Ryker and makes a grab at me. I'm *so* not having that. It's one thing to ask me if I'll go with her, another to grab me. I duck her groping hand, using my position to yank my switchblade free of my boot. Like I said, Jacksonville post-disaster era is no vacation resort. I've used a blade before, and I'm not afraid to use it again. I lash out at the woman, barely nicking the skin, but she leaps away from me.

"Stay back," Thorn barks at me, throwing out a hand to block me. His palm flattens over my chest, and he holds me back while Ryker jumps in with his dagger. Rocco swirls his hands in the air, summoning some kind of magic. I wish I could stop and watch, since I've never seen a sorcerer do magic except on TV. But I'm busy ducking around Thorn and trying to get at this lady. She started this, and I'm going to end it.

Before I can reach her, though, Rocco throws both of his thick, muscular arms out toward the woman, throwing a ball of magic that looks like a swirling distortion in the air with sparks spiraling inside it. The woman leaps backward, but Rocco turns, his arms still outstretched, and the ball of magic connects. With a furious howl, the woman crumples to the ground. Black smoke billows around her, and a second later, when it sweeps off in the wind, nothing remains but a sooty spot on the pavement.

"Holy fuck," I say, swallowing hard. "Did you just…vaporize someone?"

"Get in the car," Ryker barks, grabbing my arm and manhandling me into the town car. The other two slide into the front and close the doors, Rocco already starting the engine.

"I need to go home and see my dad," I say, trying to pull free. "And get my stuff."

"Hell no," Ryker retorts as he pushes me across the seat and hops in beside me. "You lost that privilege."

"What about my car?" I grab at the door handle, but it's locked.

Rocco chuckles as he pulls out of the lot.

"Did you just trap me with child-safe locks?" I huff, crossing my arms over my chest.

"Don't act like a child, and I won't have to," Rocco shoots back, lowering a pair of designer shades over his eyes before adjusting the mirror to look back at me.

Refusing to acknowledge how freaking hot he looks in them, I stare out the window. For the next fifteen minutes, I ignore the three stooges and go back to worrying about my dad. These guys don't get it. They think they'll simply send a note to Silas, and he'll obey. But I know my boss better than that. If I don't come to work, he'll go straight to my house. And if I don't warn my dad first...

I swallow hard, not wanting to admit the possibility of what he'll do. Thinking of all the times he told me I'm all he has to live for. If I suddenly disappear without a trace...

When we roll to a silent stop at a light, I grab the door handle and yank so hard I'm surprised it doesn't come off.

Rocco laughs again, sending murderous thoughts rolling through my brain. "I can see why she never graduated high school," he says. "Do you really think I'm going to let you run that easily again? We've got an eye on you now, Cinderella."

"Let me out," I growl.

"Not a chance."

"I'll scream," I say, because what do I have to lose? Nothing, that's what.

Ryker scoffs. "What are you, five?"

"I have a very high-pitched scream," I warn.

"Most girls save the screaming for the end of the first date, if you know what I mean," Rocco says.

I open my mouth and let out my deafening, don't-need-an-attack-whistle shriek.

The guys all flinch, and Rocco swerves into the next lane for a second.

"Jesus Christ, you psycho," Ryker growls.

I take a deep breath to belt out the next one when my throat seems to close. I nearly choke on the scream, trying to force it out, but no sound comes even when I strain. I turn to stare at

Ryker, my hand flying to my throat. I'm breathing just fine, but when I open my mouth to cuss him out, no words come.

Rocco cracks up again. "You look like a fish out of water."

"That's better," Ryker says, turning to the window as I silently plot their deaths.

He stole my freaking voice!

Rage is like a hot coal pressed against my heart, stoking it into flames of hatred by the time we reach the Academy. There has to be somebody higher up the food chain that I can talk to about this. All I wanted was to go home. To see my dad and get my stuff like every other student. They all got to say their goodbyes. It's not just unfair to me, but unfair to my dad. He didn't ask for any of this. He doesn't even have magic.

These guys are more interested in my obedience than hearing anything I have to say. One way or another, somebody's going to listen to me, though.

After a deathly silent drive to the academy, the car stops. "Oh look, we're home. Time to get Cinderella to her closet under the stairs."

"That's Harry Potter, dumbass," Thorn says, breaking his silence for the first time since we got in the car.

Term 1: Unleashing Trials

The car doors unlock, so I fling mine open and make a run for it. This time, I'm not so lucky. Ryker is standing in front of me the next second, though I don't know how he got there. I slam into him, and he grabs me in a steel embrace.

"Welcome home, sweetheart," he says, his voice so flat it makes a mockery of the word. "Your room is all set up and ready for you."

"I have to go see my dad," I argue. "He's not safe with Silas losing his servant."

Ignoring my protests, Thorn takes my hand firmly in his large, warm one. I try not to gasp at the sensation of his skin against mine. I'm not a toucher. Not since back when we had a normal family, before my sister died and my mom turned into a run-ragged, overworked zombie. The four of us would sit piled up on the couch reading books or playing games. But since then? Human contact is a rarity, and I'm not sure how I feel about it.

On the one hand, it feels like vulnerability and intimacy that I don't want with this asshole. On the other... Oh my god, I never knew how many nerve endings existed in just one little hand. It makes me want to hold on forever, to make my whole body fit where my hand is, so every inch of my skin can feel this amazing sensation coursing though me.

Thorn strides up a set of concrete steps, dragging me into a small stone building. We step into a large but cozy common room with brown leather furniture, potted plants, a huge TV mounted on the wall, and a fireplace on one side. Down a hallway I can see doors standing open, people calling back and forth to each other, decorating their doors, talking, and laughing.

They fall silent at the sight of three swoon-worthy sorcerers dragging new meat down the hall. We stop in front of a door. Thorn pulls out a key, unlocks the door, and shoves me inside with enough force that it's clear who's in charge here—and that he's done with my antics.

"Wait." I grab the door as he starts to pull it closed. "Please. I have to go home. My dad…" My throat closes on its own this time, and to my horror, tears threaten behind my eyes.

"I'm sorry," Thorn murmurs. His eyes are unreadable, his face a complete blank as his piercing emerald gaze searches mine through the crack in the door. For a second, neither of us move. Then I realize how close we're standing, just inches apart.

So close I can smell the peppermint on his breath as it caresses my cheek.

"This is your home now," Rocco interrupts, pushing the door all the way open to pass his friend and step into my room. "There are clothes already in your drawers and closets. School uniforms, that sort of thing. You might want to shower and get out of those rags before the Bellas have you for tomorrow's breakfast."

He pauses, his eyes skating over my curves before returning to mine. "Or, you know, I could do that," he says with a sexy grin.

"Don't play with the new recruits," Ryker admonishes his brother. "They're not here for your entertainment."

"And yet, they're endlessly entertaining," Rocco says, giving me a quick wink before sauntering out of my room.

Thorn pauses instead of following the other two. "Your father is a grown man," he says. "He can take care of himself."

"You don't understand," I say, that stupid, painful tightness rising to my throat again.

Thorn crosses his arms and glares. "Try me."

"Yeah, right," I blurt out before I can stop myself. But I'm not about to spill my sob story to this jerk who will just use it for ammunition. His eyes are anything but kind and understanding. He may be asking for information, but he sure as hell isn't going to use it for altruistic purposes.

"Then I can't help you," he says, pivoting to leave the room.

"Wait," I cry, grabbing a handful of his shirt before I think better of it.

He tenses, his whole body going rigid, but he doesn't turn back to me.

"He'll need protection from Silas," I say quietly, hoping the other two can't overhear. Even if they do, no amount of taunting or bullying from them is worth risking Dad's safety. Let them know. Let them come at me with their best shot. I can handle all three of them.

What I can't handle is thinking I didn't do everything in my power to protect the only family I have left in this world.

Without a word, Thorn steps out of the room and pulls the door closed behind him. I sigh and rest my forehead against the heavy wood, closing my eyes and trying to get my emotions under control. I consider trying to bolt again, but when I try the knob, it won't budge. I can't tell if it's locked or if magic has sealed it shut.

"Dammit."

I bang my fist on the door once, but I don't expect anyone to open it. Slowly letting out a breath, I look around what will apparently be my room for the foreseeable future. The room, like the common room downstairs, is cozy, almost quaint. The bedframes are oak four-posters, each mattress covered with a light, cream-colored comforter with pale pink roses along the scalloped edge. A matching bedroom set, complete with a nightstand and small wooden dresser, sits on each side of the room.

Guilt overcomes me as I sit on one of the twin beds. This is so much nicer than what Dad has. There's not a mouse-chewed, synthetic blanket in sight. The floor is hardwood with a subtly patterned rug laid between the two beds instead of stained carpet. Bright afternoon sun streams through the matching curtains instead of struggling through dusty, broken blinds.

I get up to look out the window. A pretty green orchid plant in a pot sits on the sill. The window overlooks a field going into the woods. There are people hanging out even this late, talking, laughing like life doesn't suck.

I take a deep breath. Maybe mine doesn't have to, either. It's not like I'm in prison, locked door notwithstanding. It's actually a really nice room, and I don't even have to share it with a roommate. They probably don't trust anyone with the key, but hey, privacy. If they can guarantee me Dad's safety, I could really get behind this. I've always dreamed of having magic, and now I do. I'm not going to waste it pouting.

I turn to explore the rest of the new room. There's a closet and another closed door that I find attached to a bathroom with another door. I try to open it, but it's also sealed shut.

"Assholes," I mutter.

Smart assholes, but still assholes.

The bathroom, like the rest of the room, is old-fashioned but way nicer than the one at home, with a clawfoot tub, a plush rug beside it, and delicate pink, cream, and tan tiles. It appears fully stocked and ready for its new magical guests, with everything from shampoo, toothpaste, and body lotion to towels, blow dryers, and hairbrushes.

Term 1: Unleashing Trials

After thoroughly exploring the little bathroom, I return to my room and notice the mini fridge for the first time. Opening it up, I find cans of soda and an assortment of snacks. I'm so freaking hungry I tear into a bag of trail mix and scarf it down. Silas doesn't exactly feed me during workdays. Robert sneaks me food when he can, but today, I haven't eaten anything but the burnt toast I had for breakfast. I'm starving, so I polish off a bag of chips next, then gulp down a soda in no time. This girl knows how to feed herself. Feeling a bit better, I let my mind wander back to what the guys said when they stuck me in here.

Looking at my "rags" as Rocco called them, I want to huff, but he has a point. A shower would be a welcome distraction, too. Dad and I often compete for the hot water, so it'll be nice to see how long the hot water lasts here. I'm guessing no one will be using the shower this late, anyway.

Since I didn't get to pack a bag and bring my own clothes, I open the closet to see if there's anything I can wear in the meantime. Inside, I find five pristine school uniforms hanging in a row. I literally laugh out loud. It's a stereotypical schoolgirl uniform: plaid, pleated skirt, white shirt, tie and knee socks. So not my style.

Behind that are a few dresses and a pantsuit. Since I'm more of a jeans-and-leather jacket kind of girl, I leave the closet and head for the dresser. Digging through the drawers, I find T-shirts, shorts, sweats, socks and underwear, all in my size. How long have they known I was coming?

Since I can't ask right now, I shrug it off and head to the bathroom. In the shower, the water is hot. Oh my god, it feels so good, too. I close my eyes and lean my head back, letting the water wash away the stress of the crazy day. When I feel sufficiently relaxed considering the situation, I turn off the water, dry off, and toss on a T-shirt. I eye the underwear suspiciously. What if they saw that I didn't come with my own things and just filled my drawers with stuff other people left behind? Wrinkling my nose at the thought that I have no idea where the underwear came, I decide to pass.

After blow drying my hair, I step back into my room. And nearly scream.

Professor Darius is standing in the middle of the floor.

Adrenaline shoots through me, and I barely keep myself from jumping three feet into the air in shock.

"Holy fuck," I gasp, pressing a hand to my stampeding heart.

"Not sure I've ever been described that way," Professor Darius says, rubbing his hand over the bottom half of his face and smiling a little. God, he's sexy. As his eyes roam over me, from my eyes to my nipples poking at the thin fabric of the T-shirt, over the curve of my hips, down my long, bare legs, his smile melts away, and something indecipherable replaces it. My pulse quickens when he wets his lips as his gaze sweeps back up, and a tremor starts deep inside me when our eyes meet again.

No, no, no, you cannot be attracted to your professor…

Squeezing my eyes shut for a second, I can feel my cheeks turning ten shades of red as I realize I'm not wearing any underwear. I scurry over to sit on my bed and pull the T-shirt down over my knees, fighting the urge to press my knees together against the juicy tingle going on between them.

"What are you doing in here?" I ask, my voice sharp to cover my embarrassment. "What, don't I get privacy, either?"

Professor Darius appears momentarily speechless. Well, this is new. I didn't think I'd recover my senses before him. And then a thought hits me. Maybe my priestess juju is getting to him. Which gives me another quick thought, this one sending a thrill of excitement through me.

Maybe I can learn to use it to my advantage. I mean, it's not like I have anything else to work with here.

Professor Darius finally clears his throat, and his tan cheeks actually go a tiny bit pink, which makes him totally adorable in ways I wish I'd never noticed.

"I just came to tell you that the sorcery students spoke to me," he says, clearing his throat and clasping his hands in front of himself in an oddly formal gesture, as if he's addressing a judge. "I'll talk to your boss and take care of that. In the meantime, we'll send someone to watch over your father until we can work out something with Silas."

"Oh my god, thank you," I say, so much relief washing through me that I want to jump up and throw my arms around him, toucher or not. But then I remember I'm wearing nothing but a t-shirt.

Professor Darius makes a gesture that's halfway between a nod and a slight bow. "We want you to feel comfortable here and be able to focus on your studies."

"Thank you," I say, tugging on the hem of my T-shirt.

A glimmer of a smile has returned to his eyes. "Until then, don't try to run away, and let us train you. Deal?"

"Are you sure he'll be safe?"

"He'll be safe, Jade. I promise. We may even be able to let you go home to say goodbye and gather your things in a few days."

"Really?"

His eyes drop to my legs, and he swallows before jerking his gaze away. "Provided you take your full escort."

I groan, but I can't hide my smile. It's the first time all day when I feel like I can breathe easy. "Can I call my dad, at least?"

"I'll make that happen if you behave. No more running. Got it?"

"Got it."

"That's dangerous to everyone involved—most of all you," he says. "We can't have that, can we?"

I can't help but smiling back at him. "Sorry. If Dad's safe, you have nothing to worry about."

"You, more than anyone here, need to learn about your magic and how to control it. Right now, we're all you've got."

Chapter 6

"You know, it's a real shame they let the janitors around here wear the same uniforms as the students." Blonde Bella cackles as she and her posse of beauty school dropouts walk past me in the cafeteria the next morning.

Looks like day one of magic school is already starting off with a bang, but I don't let the bitches get me down. I don't even respond. After a night of sleep so deep it makes me feel almost guilty, I'm positively giddy at the prospect of going to class today instead of trudging into Silas's mansion, a luxury I haven't been afforded in two years. Surrounded by a mixture of excited newbies and pre-established cliques from high school, I spend breakfast people-watching... And noticing how many people are watching me.

Term 1: Unleashing Trials

After the day before, I don't really blame them. Half of them look mortified and hurry away, as if I intentionally made them do crazy sex acts in the Great Hall. The rest give me looks that range from curious glances to pitying looks, from scorn and disgust to hungry lust. One thing's for sure. For better or worse, everyone knows who I am today.

As upperclassmen finish breakfast, they shoulder their bags, pick up weapons, and head off in groups and pairs. At last, the only people left in the cafeteria are those in the new class—freshmen.

I can't stop the giddy grin from breaking across my face when I realize I'm one of them. I'm a freshman student of magic at the Academy of Sorcery. I can hardly keep from jumping up and doing a happy dance. I'm literally living my dream.

"You got laid," Asher cries, sliding into the chair opposite mine. Elowen slips silently into the chair beside him and nibbles at the edge of the Pop-Tart in her hand.

"What?" I ask, looking back and forth between them. "No, I didn't."

Asher arches one black, penciled and pierced eyebrow. "You sure about that? You're sitting alone and smiling like a loon."

"Oh," I say with a little laugh. "I'm just... Really happy to be here."

"Same," he admits with a grin. Then he shoots a guilty glance at Elowen and wipes off his smile. "Sorry, girl. I know you're not happy about being in the House of Necromancy, but we'll figure it out. We'll be right here with you the whole way."

"It'll turn me dark," Elowen says, barely speaking above a whisper. "Everyone is already staring at me like I'm evil. There's no way I'm strong enough to make it through four years of practicing the dark arts without it turning me bad."

"Dark magic isn't necessarily evil," Asher says.

Elowen sets down her pastry and stares at it like she's about to cry. The scattered groups in the cafeteria have started to shift restlessly when the door swings open and in strides the tall, lean, gorgeous professor from the day before. In a pair of grey pinstripe pants and a lavender dress shirt with the sleeves rolled up to show off the bottom half of his tan forearms, he looks even more swoon-worthy than the day before. Judging from the sighs that echo around the room, I'm not the only one to notice.

Term 1: Unleashing Trials

"Good morning," Professor Darius addresses the crowd, which immediately quiets the second he starts to speak. His gaze flickers over the other students and lands on me. Our eyes lock, and something in my chest does a funny little flip.

Professor Darius drags his gaze from mine and speaks to the whole room. "Welcome to your first day at the Academy of Sorcery. Yesterday, you learned that you all have magical powers. Over the next four years, you will study and practice until you have full mastery over your magic and are ready to go out into the world and use your gifts for good. Starting today, the entire freshman class will begin to learn about basic magic and how to control it. The first step in learning that control is choosing a vessel in which to safekeep your untrained magic."

"You think I can put all my magic in there and just leave it?" Elowen whispers.

I don't have the answer to that or any other part of her predicament, so I just give her hand a quick squeeze to show her I care.

"Since newly vested magical students cannot contain all that power within themselves and still maintain balance, we each have a vessel that will hold that power," Professor Darius goes on. "From here we will go to the armory, which holds all the available vessels."

A murmur of excitement goes up around the room.

"Our weapons," Asher says, nudging me and shooting me a giddy grin.

I already have a knife, so I'm a little less impressed with that aspect, but I make up for it with excitement about having somewhere to store my embarrassing magic when it recharges.

"Yes, the vessel that helps carry and wield your magic is a weapon," Professor Darius says. "You will choose from those available. Or rather, one of those available will choose you. Keep your senses on full alert, taking your time with each one that interests you. When you find your vessel, it will call to the magic of your soul."

A shiver of excitement races through me. *The magic of my soul.* The words make me almost burst. I have magic in my very soul. It's part of me, as it always has been, but now it's ready to come out and play. Ready to be weaponized and mastered. I'm vibrating with readiness.

We all stand up and file out the door, following Professor Darius toward the armory.

"How much should we bet that Jade here gets a trash can for her weapon?" Blonde Bella says to her friends as they walk past me.

"Maybe she can use the lid for a shield," says Black-Haired Bella.

"Considering her magic, she'll probably get a dildo," says Brunette Bella, and they all burst into peals of laughter.

I've had more than enough of their crap already. Before I can stop myself, my anger boils over, and I shove a Bella from behind, knocking her into the students in front of her.

She turns around and glares as her friends help steady her and cast disgusted looks my way.

I grin. "Oh gosh, I'm sorry. I must have tripped."

"You must have a death wish." Blonde Bella steps up to me, inches from my face.

"You don't scare me," I say, stepping closer, until we're toe to toe. "You want a fight, you got one."

"Whoa there, Rocky." Asher grabs my arm and pulls me away from Bella. "Don't waste your priestess energy on those ugly ducklings."

"You're lucky my friend is such a pacifist," I call to the Bellas as Asher drags me ahead.

"Don't incite her wrath," Asher says. "You'll just make more trouble for yourself."

"You're too nice," I say. "I swear, the next time she fucks with me, I'm going to put that bitch in her place."

"Take the high road," Asher says. "We're better than that."

"I'm not," I say. "She needs to learn what happens when you cross a girl who grew up in the bad part of town. I carry a knife for a reason."

"No shanking on the first day of school," Asher says with a grin. We reach the armory, a separate building with a crackle of magic surrounding it. When we step through the door, I feel it tickle across my skin. Though I can't see the magic, it's a palpable sensation, as real as feeling the sun's rays when stepping from the shade into the sunshine.

We blink in the dim interior, waiting for our eyes to adjust. When they do, we see a long row of tables set up in the center of the room. Beyond the tables, along the wall, glass cases stand open. Inside, an assortment of larger weapons is displayed—swords, staffs, bows, clubs, and other items of various sizes and materials. On the tables lie smaller instruments like knives, daggers, and throwing stars. There are other odd choices, too, like a grenade, a golden compass, and a long purple crystal along with some other random items.

The Bellas push by me, flipping their hair and casting scathing looks as they go. "Slut witch," one of them hisses as they go.

Asher links his elbow through mine, steering me away from them. "Those twats are just jealous because you're gorgeous, and you have sexy magic."

I roll my eyes. "Lucky me."

"Are you seriously telling me you don't realize how fabulous your magic is? Who wouldn't want to be irresistible to everyone?"

"Pfft. They hate me."

"Oh, please, girl," Asher says, bumping my hip with his. "You are so naïve. Your magic rocks. You just need to learn how to use it to your advantage."

"Hey, you guys," a small voice interrupts our debate. Elowen is standing there alone, and a pang of guilt goes through me. I don't know when we lost her, but somewhere along the way, she fell behind. She's so quiet I hadn't even noticed, and now I feel like shit.

"What's wrong, girlfriend?" Asher sets his hand on her shoulder.

"I don't want to be here," she says, letting out a sigh. "I just want to go home."

"You have dark magic," Asher says. "You can't go home without learning to use it. That would be even more dangerous than ours."

It's not like she'd be allowed to go home with untrained magic and live as if nothing had happened. If she left, she'd face the same fate as anyone kicked out. She'd have to work for someone more powerful than her, someone who could siphon off her magic for the rest of her life and use it for themselves. That's what happens to people who prove they're incapable of mastering and using their magic responsibly.

"I know," Elowen says, scuffing her toe on the floor. "But I don't fit in with the dark magic students."

"I'm sorry," Asher says, giving her a hug. "I know you're shy, babe. It'll take you a minute, but I'm sure you'll make friends."

"Yeah," she says, staring at the floor.

"On the bright side, you look amazing in that uniform," I say.

She doesn't even break a smile. "I don't think I can do this."

"You can do this," I say, trying to encourage her. "Screw those dark magic jerks. You do you. I know there's a strong woman in there, even if you don't show it."

Elowen gives a quiet scoff. "Yeah, right."

"You know how I know?" I say. "You could have cut me down like all those other girls who think they have to make me look bad so they can feel better about themselves. But you stuck by me even when you knew it would put you in their path. I just met you, and I already know you're worth more than all of them put together."

Elowen nods and gives me a little smile. "Thanks."

"Less chit-chat," growls a voice from behind us. "More concentration."

I turn to see Ryker prowling through the students, a sword and scabbard on his hip. I roll my eyes at my new friends, but they're gaping at Ryker like he's some kind of rock star. Super.

"One weapon, and only one weapon, is meant for you," Professor Darius says as he also wanders through the groups of students, overlooking their choices. "It will know your magic and call out to you."

I turn back to the table, trying to focus on what's there. Some of the weapons are gleaming and beautiful, while others are crude but daunting, speaking their purpose all too clearly— violence.

My fingers twitch, and I turn back to the table, a funny little thrill going through me. I scan the table, reaching for a gleaming silver dagger. But before I touch it, a shrinking feeling grips my hand, and I draw back. I scan the table, but the only thing that calls to me at all is a funny eating utensil, a mixture of a spoon and a fork. Definitely not a weapon.

I'm distracted by a breathy sigh beside me. Elowen had hefted a grisly mace that looks so heavy I'm not sure how she's going to wield it. She stares at it morosely. "This looks evil. Like my soul will be by the time I've been here four years."

She follows Asher and I as we continue searching while other students choose cool, scary weapons. So far, nothing's speaking to me.

"These are mine," Asher says, plucking up a set of nunchucks. "Perfect for this witch."

I raise my eyebrows at him. "Don't you mean wizard?"

"Bitch, please. I'm as much a witch as you are a sex goddess." With a dramatic flick of his fingers, he swooshes his hair across his forehead.

"I'm the furthest thing from a sex goddess," I say with a laugh at his antics.

Elowen laughs, too, which is a relief since I don't know how to help her gloomy mood.

Asher throws an arm around each of us. "Come on, girlfriend. Isn't there anything calling to you?"

There is, but I don't want to admit it yet because the thing calling to me is totally lame and embarrassing. I keep walking past it in hopes that something else will hold my attention, that it'll take something more badass than a spork to hold my supposedly special magic.

After walking in circles for another ten minutes, I'm one of the last students still without a weapon. Though there is this gnarly ax beside the spork... It must be that.

I reach out to grab it, but Blonde Bella swipes it first, pulling the ax into her hand, hissing at me like a snake.

"Back off, Dumpster," Bella says, cradling the ax like a baby. She raises her voice and screeches, "This bitch is trying to steal my weapon!"

Thorn appears at our side, though I hadn't even seen him in the room before. "Is there a problem?"

"She tried to steal my weapon," Bella says, her voice all gaspy and high, like I picked up the ax and threatened her with it instead of just reaching in its direction. She leans into Thorn, whose lips tighten in an expression of distaste for just one second before she looks up at him with big, moony eyes.

That bitch is barking up the wrong tree. Thorn obviously has zero interest in her damsel in distress routine.

"Enough with the drama queen act," Thorn says, detaching himself from Bella and holding her at arm's length. "You don't look injured."

I let out a quiet snort. Maybe he's not so bad after all.

Meanwhile, Rocco has strolled over, looking amused and relaxed with his hands in the pockets of his navy slacks, his uniform fitting him to tailored perfection. Dammit, why does he have to look so good when he acts so bad?

"It takes two to tango," he says, turning to me. "I don't think Bella's the only one at fault here."

"Excuse me?" I say.

Rocco smiles, making dimples sink into his cheeks. "Can't keep yourself out of trouble for five minutes, can you?"

"I didn't—." I break off, taking a deep breath to control my fury. "You know what? Never mind."

He grins wider, his gaze sweeping over me and Bella. "As much fun as it would be to see two girls wrestling, I'd rather it be a private show with a lot more body oil and a lot less clothes."

He's so ridiculous that it's hard to even stay mad at him. I try not to laugh, instead rolling my eyes as I say, "Keep dreaming, dumbass."

"Oh, I plan on it," Rocco says, letting his eyes rake down my body this time.

I flip my hair over my shoulder and walk away with my head held high. Asher follows, snickering. I keep wandering around the room, searching desperately for any weapon not in the form of a spork. I mean, seriously. A spork isn't even a real thing. It's the ugly stepchild of eating utensils. Who the hell would intentionally choose it for anything other than a joke?

But literally nothing else has called to me.

I let out a sigh as I pass the silver spork for the fifth time, begging the universe for a sign that there is another weapon out there that belongs to me. I can't pick a spork. I'll be the laughing stock of the school.

Within five more minutes, everyone has chosen a weapon but me.

"Today, Cinderella," Rocco calls out from across the room.

Professor Darius slowly approaches, his hands clasped behind his back. He stops beside me, where I stand staring at the spork. His elbow lightly brushes against mine, and a tingle goes racing through me. I am seriously lusting after this man.

When I peek at him from the corner of my eye, he closes his eyes and takes a long, slow breath before opening his lids again.

"Anything calling to you?" he asks.

Yeah. *He's* calling to me. Does that count?

"Nope," I lie.

A spork is so not my weapon of choice. It's not even my eating utensil of choice.

We start walking, and all the while, I revel in this strange vibration I'm getting from him.

"Concentrate," he murmurs. "Let your magic guide you. Where is it drawing you?"

I suddenly realize everyone in the entire armory is watching us. Waiting for the big reveal. Not only am I the wielder of sex-magic that made them do embarrassing things, now I'm making a spectacle of myself by not choosing a weapon.

If only I'd grabbed it while everyone was busy looking for their own weapon.

Taking a deep breath, I swallow down my ever-growing embarrassment and point to the spork. A ripple of hushed conversation sweeps over the gathering of freshmen as they strain to see what I've pointed to. It's so small that not many people can even see it from their vantage point near the door as they wait to leave.

Professor Darius nods gravely. "You're certain?"

"I wish I wasn't," I say with a sigh. I close my eyes one last time and strain to feel a pull toward anything else, but there's nothing but an insistent, nagging itch to pick up the damn spork.

"This has been here for many years," Professor Darius muses, picking up the spork. "Since before I was a student at Academy of Sorcery."

I fight an almost uncontrollable urge to snatch the thing from his hand. It's *mine*.

No, ours. Mine and my magic's.

"Can I please have it?" I ask, holding out a hand and forcing my voice not to betray my desperation.

"It's yours," he says, laying it across my palm like it's something worthy of reverence. "Receive your weapon."

By now, everyone has seen the ridiculous "weapon," and the whole room erupts into giggles and outright guffaws. Haha, everybody look at the sex magnet wielding a spork. Super.

"Piss off," I say to everyone as I storm past them and out of the armory. Thanks to my magic, which seems intent on making my life hell, I can't even get a minute alone to lick my wounds. I have a trio of sorcerers following me around.

"Nice spork," Rocco says behind me. "Better be careful with that, don't want to poke your eye out."

Ryker breaks into laughter.

"I don't need this shit," I say, turning to glare at the assholes laughing at me. I stomp over and toss the spork into a trashcan. "And I don't need that. I'm out of here."

Chapter 7

"Good morning, everyone," Professor Darius says the next day as he strides into my first class of the day, Basics of Magic. "As you know, I'm the head of the College of Wizardry, which means you're stuck with me for the next four years. If you have any questions, I'm your touch-point." His eyes find mine, and a rush of warmth fills my chest. It's official. I'm crushing hard.

"In this class, you'll learn how to begin controlling your magic and using it to your advantage," Professor Darius goes on. "But in order for that to happen, you'll need to store most of it in your vessel for now. That way, you can work with a small amount that is safe and won't cause serious injury if it gets away from you. Don't worry, your magic will be safely kept in your weapon or other instrument of choice. You can pull from it anytime you need more magic."

While he talks, he walks around the room, and all the students take out their weapons and hold them out in front of them.

Everybody but me.

"I want you to think of it like an extension of yourself, with magic flowing freely between you and your vessel," Professor Darius continues, holding out what looks like sleek walnut cane with a snake's head at the tip. A blade with two points flicks out the end like a tongue before drawing back in. "This is mine, and although I no longer need it, I'm very attached to it, as you will be once you've bonded with yours. Today, we're going to work on getting your magic safely stored. In the coming weeks, we'll work on transferring it back and forth until you're fully in control of the process and sharing your magic with your weapon and knowing how much to draw from it is second nature."

"How much magic do you have?" asks a guy in the back.

Professor Darius smiles a bit. "Enough," he answers, pausing next to Brunette Bella, who looks like she's about to wet herself with adoration as she stares up at him. "We all have special relationships with our weapons. Your particular weapon, each unique to the wizard who wields it, chose you for a reason. You will use it to learn balance. Too much magic at any given time can overwhelm us, causing imbalances of power and hurting ourselves and those around us."

My gaze wanders around the room to all the students concentrating on their weapons while I stand here like an idiot, holding nothing because I was a dumbass and tossed mine in the trash when I was pissed. Hopefully I can replace it with something not quite as lame as a spork, and it will all be forgotten.

I cross my arms over my chest and exhale, annoyed at both myself and the damn spork that insisted it was my weapon. The only magic that thing could deliver is dessert. Not to say that a bowl of ice cream at the right moment isn't magical. Let's face it, it's gotten me through a few tough spots. But I don't think it's going to save me from being the butt of every joke this year, let alone an actual attacker.

"Where'd your spork go, Dumpster?" Blonde Bella mocks me. "Couldn't handle it? I'm not surprised, really. With your magic, what are you going to do, seduce it?"

"I was actually looking forward to seeing her try to fight someone with it," Brunette Bella says.

"Too bad I'm getting something else," I say. "I could have gouged your eye out with it."

"Where is your weapon, Jade?" Professor Darius asks. I hadn't noticed him walking over, but now he's standing right next to me, so close I can smell his spicy aftershave. The neurons in my brain all start firing at once, and I can't find a single clever thing to say. I can only shrug.

"You won't be able to use your magic without it," he says. "Can you go back to your room to get it?"

"I kind of… Threw it away," I mumble beneath my breath.

"You threw it away?" He gives me this look of disappointment. Unlike my three chaperones, whose opinions I could care less about, Professor Darius's disappointment stings. "That weapon's been waiting for the right person for decades, Jade. For someone special enough to choose it despite

109

its lowly appearance. That weapon can contain great power such as yours."

"It's a spork," I argue. "How am I supposed to be a serious magician with a spork? Can't I choose something else?"

"A vessel is more than it seems," he says. "It chose you for a reason, the same reason your magic chose it." He leans closer, and the scent of his aftershave makes me dizzy. His eyes are locked on mine, the gold flecks in his chocolate irises mesmerizing me. He drops his voice, still holding my gaze. "Go find it."

A shiver races through me, and I'm not sure if it's attraction or fear that I've pissed off the most powerful man in the entire school. Avoiding the eyes of my classmates, I rush out of the room and try to collect myself and catch my breath as I return to the trash can. I take off the top of the can and start digging through the coffee cups and gum wrappers in search of the stupid spork.

Rocco strolls up behind me, his hands in his pockets, and stands there just grinning while I dig through the refuse in vain. Finally, I sit back on my heel and wipe my forehead with the back of my wrist, brushing my blonde hair aside. I glare up at

Rocco, who raises his eyebrows but for once stays blessedly silent.

"What are you staring at?" I ask.

"You have gum on your sleeve," he points out.

A wad of chewed gum is glued to the white sleeve of my uniform. I mutter a curse, stand up, and stride toward my dorm, Rocco following behind me on guard duty. When I reach my room, I take great pleasure in slamming the door in his face.

Chapter 8

Week one and two blur by after that. I have to sit through Professor Darius's disappointed frown each day when I show up without a weapon, but I listen to the lessons and take meticulous notes so I can practice once I get a replacement weapon. Nothing in the armory wants my magic, though, even after a couple visits to try for a replacement. Since I didn't put any magic in the spork yet, it's not a great danger that it's gone, but it's definitely a great annoyance.

The school is divided into houses, each one specializing in one kind of magic—wizards, witches, conjurers, and so on— but there's only one priestess, so I joined House of Wizardry since it's where my only friend is assigned. Besides Basics of Magic, I don't have any classes with Professor Darius.

Term 1: Unleashing Trials

Supernatural Law class is a snooze fest until the teacher starts talking about the various loopholes in the law. Apparently, the Silas situation happens from time to time when corrupt courts allow ridiculous contracts that pretty much amount to forced servitude for people like my mother. And me. It's happened to vampires, werewolves, and other supernaturals as well, people with much more magic who are much harder to control than my psychic mother. Lucky for me, Thorn, who's my guard during this class, points out to the teacher that there's an example right here. And then everyone stares at me while the teacher dissects my mother's case in front of the whole class.

Spell-casting is tons better, even though I have to suffer through having Rocco in there with me. Still, I get a wand like everyone else, and once they explain that any magic can be channeled once we learn the spells, I throw myself into it with all I have. If I can't do magic with my spork, at least the wand lets me use some of it. Once I get the hang of it, I'm pretty badass at wand wielding. Too bad they forbid students from practicing on humans.

My favorite class is my last class of the day, though—hand-to-hand combat, where Asher immediately grabs me as a partner on the first day, and after that, it's a given that we'll pair up every day. As we're leaving our class on Friday, I spot Elowen leaning on the wall outside the dark arts wing, chewing on her nails and staring off into space.

"Have you talked to Elowen this week?" I ask Asher. "She doesn't look so good."

Asher looks over and purses his lips. "Since she's in the dark magic wing of the school, I haven't seen much of her. She's been distant when I tried."

"Come on, let's go check on her." I nudge him, and he follows me across the grass to our friend.

Asher gives her a hug when we reach her. "How you holding up, girl?"

Elowen shrugs and avoids our eyes. "I've protested, begged, done everything I can think of to get out of here, but nothing's helped." Her voice cracks, and tears cling to her long lashes.

"There must be something we can do," I say, hating to see her in pain.

"There's not," she says, her voice full of defeat. "I can feel it happening already. I'm going dark, Jade. I can't stop it."

"There's always a choice," I say firmly. "You can't choose your magic, but you can control what you do with it."

The Bellas start across the grass, walking toward the dorm.

"I have to go," Elowen says before turning to dart back into the building where her classes are held.

"Look at her, scurrying away like a little rat," Black-Haired Bella says with a sneer.

"She *looks* like a rat," Brunette Bella says, speaking loudly enough that we can hear her as she walks away with her posse, their mean laughter echoing harshly through the sunny campus.

That night, as I lie in my bed, I can't sleep. It's the second weekend I'll spend away from home, and the truth is, I miss my dad more, not less. True to his word, Professor Darius let me make a call to talk to my dad, so at least he won't be worrying himself to death not knowing where I am. He assured me he was fine, but I can't help but worry. What if he was saying it just to put my mind at ease so I could focus on studying?

Letting out a sigh, I sit up and throw off my blankets. I need to see Dad for myself, to make sure he's okay and that Silas isn't bothering him. They haven't let me go, since I can't find my spork to store my magic. But I can feel my magic growing stronger, just like Elowen. The longer I wait, the more dangerous it will be to go home. I need to go now, before it gets too strong.

I don't have a car here, but I'm resourceful. I'll figure something out.

After pulling on some black jeans and a black tee, I shove my feet in my boots and grab my keys. I've been warned about my magic, and how dangerous it could be to leave the school, but it's been a week and so far, not much has happened even with it increasing again. It's not like guys are following me around sexually harassing me and refusing to take no for an answer. The other students seem more weirded out by me than attracted to me. And I've lived in the bad part of Jacksonville all my life. Maybe I don't know about magic, but I can handle myself on the streets. I have a knife in my boot. I don't need a freaking spork.

As quietly as I can, I pull open the door and peer up and down the deserted hallway. It's dark, though there are wall sconces flickering at the ends near the stairwells. Perfect. Closing the door behind me, I tiptoe down the hallway to the stairwell and step into the light.

Thorn is standing on the second step, leaning against the wall with one foot propped on the wall behind him. When he sees me, he raises an eyebrow, looking so bored I wonder if he can't be bothered to lift both brows. "Where do you think you're going?" he asks, not sounding at all surprised to see me.

I'm startled to find him there, though. For a second, I'm mesmerized by his haunting green eyes. They contrast like art with his ebony hair that's swept over his forehead.

Then I remember that I hate him. "What are *you* doing here?" I demand.

"I have guard duty tonight. You didn't think we left you alone at night, did you?"

"So not only do you guys follow me around all day, you're also stalking my room at night?"

"And for good reason, it seems," he says, his eyes flicking to my keys.

"I need to see my dad," I say, squaring my shoulders. "I have a right to say goodbye to my family, just like everyone else here got to do. And I need to make sure Silas is really okay with me not coming back right now."

"We're taking care of your boss. Didn't Darius tell you not to worry about that?"

"Well, yeah," I admit. "But why would I trust any of you?"

"You can trust us," he says. "He said don't worry about it. That means don't worry about it."

"I don't know who to trust around here," I admit, sagging against the wall. I realize I'm sharing something with him instead of just trading barbed comments, but I'm too frustrated to care right now.

Thorn considers and then blows out a breath. "I get it. But you need to understand we're guarding you for *your* protection. You have no idea what could happen if you let your magic go unchecked. Chaos, like you saw at the Unleashing. Is that what you want?"

"No," I say, slumping in defeat.

"It's not my first choice of ways to spend Friday night, either," he says, his emerald eyes going frosty as he crosses his arms over his chest. I can't help but notice the defined muscles showing through his white T-shirt. Yum.

I pull my eyes away and straighten from the wall. "Believe me, I'm as sorry as you are for the circumstances," I say. "So, what do you say we make a truce?"

He narrows his eyes and studies me, and I realize my heart is pounding as I wait for his answer. I hold out a hand, and after a long moment when I'm sure he's going to grab it and cuff me to the railing on the stairs, he uncrosses his arms and joins his hand with mine.

A jolt rocks through me when his warm skin connects with mine in a firm hold. I forgot how insane touching people makes me now that I have this sexy magic. Thorn quickly wets his lips. "Truce," he says, not releasing my hand.

I raise my eyes from our linked hands to his gemlike gaze. For one second, I can see my own turbulent emotions reflected back at me, and I realize he's affected by me in the same way I'm affected by him.

He yanks his hand back and crosses his arms across his chest again. "Was that a trick?" he asks, a fierce scowl on his face.

"What? No," I say. "I… I'm sorry." I cross my own arms, feeling a mixture of defensive and awkward.

"You understand why I have to say no. It's not safe for you out there."

"What if you came with me?" I ask. "You can make sure I'm safe, and I can get my stuff and see my dad."

"You shouldn't be alone with any man," Thorn says. "Not even me."

"I'm alone with you right now," I point out.

Thorn works his bottom lip with his teeth, something I can't help but stare at as that sharp white edge worries his plump lower lip. Finally he shoves his hand in his jeans pocket, and I can hear his keys jangling. "You have thirty minutes, got it? Go in, see your dad, grab some stuff and we leave. No more."

Happiness fills me at the thought of seeing my dad again, and I can't help the grin that spreads across my face. "You know, just when I decide I hate you guys, you go and do something redeeming, and I change my mind."

"Well, don't." He grabs my forearm and gently pulls me down the stairs with him. "There's no redeeming any of us, and it'd be best if you remember that when you think otherwise."

Unsure what he means by that, I decide to shrug it off and appreciate his generosity before he changes his mind. As we cross the parking lot, I change the subject. "Why can't I have my car?"

"Because of this." He waves his arm as we walk beneath a light illuminating the small lot. "If you had a car, you'd bolt at the first opportunity. We obviously can't trust you. I mean, how were you planning on getting home, anyway? You have no cell, no money."

I shrug. "I'd figure it out."

"What were you, a car thief in your former life?"

"I know things," I say. "So what?"

Thorn just shakes his head and strides over to a shiny black sports car. I don't know much about cars, but I know fast when I see it. Shiny silver wheels and low-profile tires sit tightly under swoopy, curved fenders. It has a spoiler in the back, but it doesn't look cheesy like some cars that have them. It belongs here, somehow.

He unlocks the door and turns to me. "Where do you live?"

When I give him my address, his eyes nearly bug out of his head. "Are you fucking kidding? You wanted to go there in the middle of the night? Alone?"

"Don't underestimate me," I say simply, then slide into the sleek leather passenger seat.

Thorn slides in behind the wheel. For a brief second, he looks at me with something I don't recognize. But then the scowl returns, and he starts up his car.

"Don't touch anything," he growls. "And lock your damn door."

He drives us up I-95 after a few minutes, and then turns off at an exit just north of the downtown area. The pond at Brentwood Park shines in the murky night air off to our left. Sandy sidewalks and palm trees line the streets, along with cars that have mostly seen better days. The occasional convenience store lights up the night with a glow of neon, and we wind through the streets of my old neighborhood.

Though my pulse is erratic with anticipation, I can't help but notice the shabbiness of the apartment buildings, as if seeing them for the first time. After only a week away, it looks foreign somehow—both depressing and frightening, with figures lurking in the shadows, desperate humans hawking their blood to desperate vampires, and displaced shifters curled in alleyways or digging through trash cans for scraps. And though all these things are commonplace, they seem different now. It's as if I'm seeing the neighborhood the way Thorn must see it.

We arrive outside our apartment building and pull up along the curb.

I move to open the door, but Thorn grabs my wrist and stops me. "Thirty minutes. Understand? No bullshit. I'm risking my ass for you, Jade."

I nod, a lump in my throat. I don't know what happened to his family, but between the look on his face last time I asked to see my dad, and the risk he's taking right now, I know he understands this somehow. He's lost people, too. He knows how much this means to me.

"Thank you."

"Get your shit, say goodbye to your dad, and that's it."

"I promise, I won't bail on you."

"All right, clock's ticking. Let's go."

We both get out of the car and head for the door to our apartment. When we walk in, the place is hot and stuffy, but the light is on in the kitchen. Dad appears in the doorway a second later. He looks terrible, his skin dull, his eyes sunken. His salt and pepper hair seems more salt than pepper. He pulls me into a hug. "Thank god you're all right."

"You, too," I say, my voice muffled in his shirt. I'm glad Thorn can't see the tears dampening my lashes.

Dad ushers me and Thorn inside and then closes and locks the door behind him. "Who's this?"

"This is Thorn. One of the older students at the academy. He's my bodyguard."

I shoot Thorn a look to see if he'll protest that statement, since it makes it sound like he works for me, but he only holds out a hand to shake Dad's.

"Why do you need a bodyguard?" Dad asks, looking confused.

I let out a sigh. "For the same reason you do. It seems my magic is powerful, and there are people who may want to hurt me because of it. Also, because we've pissed off Silas. They need to protect us both."

"That man," Dad grumbles.

I hug him one more time, because even though we're not huggers, this might be the last time for a while. I fight back more tears as I squeeze his frail frame. "I'd love to stick around, but I only have thirty minutes," I say, releasing my father.

"Twenty-six," Thorn says.

"I need to grab a few things, like my phone." I glare at the gorgeous sorcerer guarding the front door, then motion for dad to follow as I walk down the small hallway and into my bedroom. I flip on the light and glance around my room, exactly as I left it two weeks ago. Though I miss my dad, I have to admit the thought of returning to this gloomy house fills me with dread. Life at the academy may not be the fantasy I had in mind all those years, but it's nice to have clean sheets, new clothes, and decent food. Knowing Dad's safe makes the burden of guilt a bit less. If I came home to live, it would put him in danger. He's better off with me at the academy.

While Dad goes to get a bag, I grab my undergarments, a few favorite outfits, and my phone. I stuff them in the bag as Thorn's voice echoes through the apartment.

"Fifteen minutes."

I head to the bathroom and toss in what little make-up and toiletries that I have. A couple minutes later, I return to my room for one last thing. It's a picture of Mom, Dad, Autumn, and me, the last one of the four of us I have. It was taken the year before Autumn died.

I carefully wrap it in my favorite nightshirt and stuff it in my duffle. Then I pick up my pillow and shove it under my arm. I find Dad and Thorn standing in the living room not talking.

"You look tired," I say to Dad. "Are you sleeping okay?"

"I'll sleep better tonight," he says, setting his hands on my shoulders. "But you shouldn't have come. Thorn says it could be dangerous for you to visit."

I glare over his shoulder at the sorcerer. "You know I can take care of myself."

"Yes," Dad says, looking sad and worn out. "You've been doing that since your mother died."

I scowl at him, not wanting Thorn to know any personal details about me. But then, he already knows about Mom. Everyone in the magical community does. It just feels more personal, somehow, to have him hear it from my father.

"I'm more worried about you," I say to Dad. "Will you be okay?"

"I'll be fine," he says. "Please don't take unnecessary risks, Jade. I can't lose you, too."

"I won't," I promise.

"Five minutes," Thorn warns.

I want to scream at him, to throw something, to tell him what an asshole he's being. But he doesn't care what I think of him or what I say. All he cares about is the time and saving his own ass from getting in trouble with the headmaster.

"You better get back," Dad says.

With a nod, I give Dad one last hug and turn to where Thorn is standing at the door, jingling his keys—his not-so-subtle ways of telling me time's up.

"I'll call soon, okay?" I say to Dad. "Take care. Love you."

"You, too. Stay safe."

I want to say more, so much more, but my throat is choked with unshed tears, and I don't want to show more weakness in front of Thorn. I gather my emotions and stride out the door that Thorn is holding open. I turn around to take one last look at my dad, but he's already closed the door.

Fighting to control my tears, I follow Thorn to his car and toss my stuff into the back seat. As I close the door, a shadow whips by me in the night.

"Did you see that?" I ask, spinning so my back is to the car.

Thorn's voice is tight. "Get in the car, Jade. Now."

I reach out for the car door, but before I can pull it open, something slams into me. I hit the ground, skinning my palms on the concrete as I catch myself. Then I see her.

The raven-haired beauty stands over me. She's tall, thin and very intimidating. Her wide eyes glow out at me from the darkness.

I jump to my feet and bend to snatch my knife from my boot. The woman is too fast, and before I have a chance to strike, she knocks the blade away with a swish of her hand.

"Takes a lot of guts to attack a helpless newbie," Thorn snarls, leaping at the woman.

She spins out of his path, twisting around to shoot black energy out of her hands as she blurs across the lot. The magic hits Thorn in the chest, slamming him to the ground. Instead of rising, he begins to slide across the concrete toward her as she makes a motion like pulling an invisible rope, reeling him in. He struggles to free himself, but she keeps pulling him.

"Thorn," I cry, racing toward him. He reaches in his pocket, twists around, and throws me something.

I catch it without thinking and stare down at my spork.

I don't have long to think about it, though. The woman has pounced on my protector.

"Pour your magic into it," Thorn yells at me as the woman strikes him in the neck.

"How?" I scream, too desperate to remember the methodical lessons Professor Darius taught us.

Thorn doesn't answer. He throws up a hand, blocking the woman's next volley of magic. She shrieks in anger as the blur of magic shoots into the sky instead of him.

I close my eyes and squeeze my hand around the handle of the spork, trying to will my magic into it. For a second I'm distracted by the grooves in the back of it, a design etched in that I never even looked at in my hurry to toss it and end my humiliation. Now it's my only hope.

I concentrate hard, visualizing my magical energy as this blue light. A tingling sensation spreads down my arm, and I can feel the moment it pours into the spork.

"Please don't make us sex crazed nymphomaniacs," I say beneath my breath as I open my eyes to check how Thorn is faring.

He's still fighting, but I can see the lines of pain etched across his face as the woman appears to have some kind of strangling spell on him, squeezing him tighter and tighter. His nose is bleeding, and I'm pretty sure I can see trickles of blood coming from his ears as well.

Shit. I run over to them, desperate to get this witch-lady off my protector. Without thinking, I use my spork like it's as mighty as any other weapon. I thrust it at her, imagining impaling her with a short sword instead of an eating utensil. The next second, I'm plunging that short sword into the woman's chest. She screams, falling backward off Thorn and clutching her chest. Thorn scrambles to his knees, but before we can grab her, the woman disappears in a puff of black smoke.

I stare at the sword in my hand, which is smeared with black blood.

"What the fuck just happened?" I ask as the last trace of smoke disappears into the darkness around us.

Thorn grunts in response. His head is bent, and blood is dripping from his face to the concrete.

"What do I do?" I ask, glancing around. Passing vampires and shifters are sure to smell the blood and come running.

"I'm fine."

"Let me help you." I rise to my feet and grab his hand, pulling him up. "Give me your keys."

"You're not driving my car."

"Uh, yeah. I am. Look at you." He barely has enough energy to stand on his own much less drive. "You're in no shape to drive, and we need to get out of here."

Thorn glances around, his green eyes flashing with recognition, like he's just realizing we're not at the academy anymore. A scuffling sound in an alley seems to make up his mind. He digs in his pocket, pulls out his keys, and smacks them into my palm. "If you wreck my car, I'll kill you myself."

We climb into the car, and I start it up. It purrs to life like a kitten. This is going to be fun.

Thorn leans forward, resting his forehead on the dashboard as he clutches his sides, his arms wrapped around himself.

Okay, less fun than I imagined. But I've never driven anything but an old junker, and Thorn's BMW is no lemon. Plus, I got to see my dad, who is safe, I got a few things from home, and I got back my spork. I even managed to use it to fight off a demon lady or whatever she is. All in all, I'd call this a productive night. I just wish I didn't have to worry that I'm going to arrive back at the academy with a dead sorcerer in the passenger seat.

For the next twenty minutes, I drive back to the Academy in silence.

When we're almost there, I turn to Thorn. "How long have you had my spork?"

"Since you threw it away," he says, not lifting his head. "I figured you'd need it back."

"And you were just going to let me go to class and disappoint the professor every day until… When, exactly? When were you planning to give it back?"

"When you asked us about it," he said.

"Has anyone ever told you that you're a real piece of work?"

He lets out a little breath that I'm pretty sure is laughter, but I can't see his face so I can't be sure. "And you're a real brat."

"I prefer the term badass," I say. "Although stubborn is acceptable if you have to insult me."

Thorn doesn't respond. When we pull into the parking lot, Rocco and Ryker stand with arms folded across their chests, waiting for us.

Chapter 9

"What the fuck were you thinking?" Ryker asks, grabbing Thorn when he stumbles out of the car.

"He's hurt, leave him alone," I say. "All he did was help me. If you're going to be pissed at someone, you can be pissed at me."

Ryker turns blazing eyes my way. "Oh, trust me, I'm plenty angry at you."

Angry doesn't begin to cover his expression, but before I can explain further, Rocco grabs my arm and drags me toward the dorm.

"Hey, let me go," I protest, but he pays no attention. I twist around to see Thorn throw an arm over Ryker's shoulder. Ryker puts an arm around Thorn for support, and together they head off in the other direction, hopefully to see whatever doctor works on campus.

"Maybe you need a guard inside your room," Rocco says. "I volunteer, on the condition that you walk around your room naked at least fifty percent of the time."

"You watch too much porn."

"What's porn?" he asks with a grin. "I just want to see you naked."

"I'm surprised there's not a Cinderella joke in there somewhere," I say, rolling my eyes. "Maybe something about how I should wear one of those cheesy maid costumes to work?"

Rocco's eyes light up. "I knew we'd eventually see eye to eye."

I can't help but laugh. I want to hate him, but as irritating as he is, he's just so over the top that I can't help but laugh at his antics. I realize with a shock of horror that I usually walk away from our interactions smiling. Crap. Have his dimples gotten to me?

He stops outside my room and leans down, resting his forearm on the wall over my head. "Want me to come in?" he asks, his voice low and sexy, his eyes smoldering. Only the smile twitching the corner of his lips belies his true intention. "I bet you could use the company after what you've been through. I'm a great distraction."

God, he really would be. A little thrill goes through me when I think of those big, strong arms around me all night. He could probably pick me up like I weigh nothing, toss me around…

And then I remember that I hate him, and I push him away, my cheeks warming. I can't help but notice, though, how hard the muscles in his chest are when I press my palm against them, how warm his body feels, and the way his dimples sink into his cheeks when he laughs and steps away from me.

"Goodnight, Rocco," I say.

He slips a hand behind my head and pulls me in, and for one split second, adrenaline charges through me and my heart flips over in my chest. Rocco presses his lips to my forehead before releasing me. "Goodnight, Cinderella."

I don't know what's happening to me. I fumble my keys and drop them, and Rocco chuckles when I have to retrieve them off the floor and try a second time before I can get into my room. I dart inside and close the door, then fall back against it and close my eyes, trying to get my breathing under control. But my breathing is not the problem. My hormones seem to be going wild. Or my libido. Or something.

I blame it on the magic. That must be it. My magic is fucking with my head again. There's no other explanation. There's no way I'd be attracted to such assholes if it wasn't for that. Because I'm not just attracted to Rocco. I'm attracted to Thorn, too. Not to mention I'm still crushing on Professor Darius. Yep. It's totally the magic.

I wish I could convince myself that's all it is.

Chapter 10

I'm rudely awakened by someone storming into my room first thing Monday morning.

"Get up," Ryker barks, yanking my blanket off. "You're late for class."

I groan and bury my head in the pillow. "What ungodly hour is it? I just fell asleep."

"Think about that the next time you want to take off in the middle of the night," he says, tossing a uniform onto the bed. It falls on my bare legs, reminding me that I'm only wearing underwear and a T-shirt, and he's seeing more of me than anyone has since… Ever.

"Get up." He stands over the bed looking down at me with barely restrained fury. "Now."

I'm too tired to fight, so I drag myself out of bed, spend five minutes in the bathroom, and then follow Ryker out of the dorm.

He shoves my spork at me, and I grab it and hold it close to my body, suddenly angry. Not only did he touch my weapon, he's walking so fast I have to nearly run to keep up, chasing after him like one of his desperate fangirls.

"Would you slow down?" I demand, almost out of breath as I run a few steps to catch him.

"We're late," he says, not even looking at me.

"Where are we even going?" I ask. "I don't have a class this early."

"You do now."

He opens the door to a classroom and strides in, and the protest dies on my lips when I see a large room with rubber flooring and a small gathering of students waiting. They each hold a sword, and they all turn to the door as we enter.

"Sorry for the delay," Ryker says, stopping in front of the class.

"You have got to be kidding," I mutter.

Black-Haired Bella gives me the evil eye stare down.

"Now that Jade has graced us with her presence, we can start class," Ryker says, glaring daggers at me.

"What's she going to do, stab us with her spork?" Bella asks with a sneer.

"Focus on your partners," Ryker says to the class.

When everyone starts sparring, he stalks over to me. "Get out your weapon."

"You're a teacher?" I ask. "I thought you were a student."

"I'm a grad student," he says. "I'm also the best swordsman in the academy. Which means that now that you've figured out your weapon, I'm your instructor."

"Guess it's my lucky day," I mutter, brandishing my spork.

"Damn right, it is," Ryker snaps, his blue eyes flashing. "If it wasn't, you'd be out on your ass after the stunt you pulled Friday night."

"Is he okay?" I ask, glancing at the other students. But they're all busy sparring, which means I have Ryker to myself.

"You're weeks behind in your training," Ryker says, stalking forward. He swipes at me, and I jump back with a yelp.

"No thanks to any of you," I say. "Since you knew where my weapon was all along."

"Treat your weapon like an extension of yourself," Ryker says, swiping at me again. I slash back at him with my sad little spork, willing it to change into a sword.

It doesn't.

"Your weapon is your best friend, your teammate, your soulmate," Ryker says, slicing at me again. This time, he makes a clean swipe through my skirt, leaving it half as long as it was before. Which means I'm pretty close to flashing my entire class every time I move.

Ryker doesn't even stop to laugh. He jabs at me again, sending me scurrying out of his way.

"You need to bond with your weapon like it has a mind of its own. It's a magical relic, so it actually does. Which is why you don't throw them in the garbage."

"That's why it's not coming out right now?" I ask. "Because I offended it?"

I jump back, but Ryker is too fast. He swipes my legs out from under me, and I fall flat. What little is left of my skirt flies up, and I flash the entire class a view of the worn-out old underwear I retrieved from home the other night.

Everyone in the room laughs. Bella doubles over with her hands on her knees, howling and pointing to make sure everyone sees. "Did you get those at the thrift shop, or while you were out Dumpster diving?" she cackles.

"Get up," Ryker says. He stands over me, brandishing his sword while everyone laughs. He doesn't laugh. But he also doesn't look like he gives a single fuck that he just made a laughingstock of me even more than my spork did.

Because I'm not suicidal, and he's holding a blade pointed at my heart, I scramble to my feet, humiliation raging through me. I clasp my spork between two hands, which makes Bella snort even louder. Now that we've drawn attention, everyone stops to watch.

Ignoring their stares, I swallow back the fist of tightness lodged in my throat. I won't let them win. I focus on my fury instead of my humiliation as I try to replicate what I did last night by visualizing what I want the spork to be.

I feel a vibration of magic, and triumph blooms inside me. The spork begins to buzz in my hand, and the next moment, a shimmer of magic surrounds the utensil. I'm doing it! I'm transferring my magic.

In a burst of light, the spork transforms.

Into a rubber hose.

It dangles from my hand like a limp, impotent dick.

This time, the laughter is even more raucous. The knot in my throat chokes off my air, and I turn and run for the door. Before I reach it, Ryker appears in front of me, blocking my path.

"Get the fuck out of my way," I hiss, shaking the length of hose at him.

Behind me, people are rolling with laughter.

"Is that all it takes to make you quit?" Ryker asks. "A little mishap with your weapon, and you're ready to run away and hide? I thought you wanted to learn magic."

"I do," I say, shoving my way past him. "But I don't see anyone else having to do this shit."

"You think you're the only person here who's had a hard life?" he asks. "Look around you, Jade. Everyone in this room has struggles. Not just you."

I pause at the door. He's right. No one else is running. And I won't run, either. Let them laugh now. The bitches won't win. I won't let them. Not this time.

I turn back to Ryker. "Fine," I say. "Teach me."

But it's a little hard for a swordsmanship teacher to teach someone without a sword. And my spork seems determined to be anything but a sword. Ryker rides my ass the entire class, but it doesn't help. My spork will not cooperate. I'm about ready to toss it in the trash again because it clearly hates me.

"Let's go, Jade. Class is almost over, and you haven't even started," Ryker barks. "Quit playing around."

If I had a sword, I'd shove it down his fucking throat right now. I focus as hard as I can, and... It turns into a broom.

"Hey, look," Bella jeers. "The janitor finally has a tool she can actually use."

"Yeah, maybe I can use it to sweep off your ass," I say. "I hear it gets a lot of use."

Bella dives at me, screeching, "Bring it, bitch."

Ryker steps between us and holds out his arms, holding us apart. "That's enough," he growls. "Class dismissed. Everyone except Jade."

Bella scoffs, flips her hair at me, and stomps off out of the room with the rest of the class. My jaw drops, and I start to protest, but Ryker shuts me down.

"You're going to get yourself killed if you don't learn to control your magic," he says as if he didn't even notice the fight that almost happened in his class. "Now do it."

"I'm going to be late for Professor Darius's class," I protest.

"I said, make your sword," he says, his eyes narrowed with fury. The rest of the class is gone, and all I want is to go ask Professor Darius how to transfer magic, because I obviously missed something despite my meticulous note-taking. But Ryker looks like he wants nothing more than an excuse to bind my magic and kick me out of the academy for good. I don't trust him not to rat me out for Friday night's excursion if I don't do what he wants, so I sigh and try again.

I spend the next twenty minutes doing the exact same thing. The spork continues to do nothing but embarrass me. I get so pissed that I scream in frustration, but it is not swayed.

Ryker holds out his sword with two hands, ready to strike. "Weapons up," he warns. "Unless you want to die."

Picking up the spork, which is currently shaped like a crowbar, I close my eyes and focus, imagining a long sword, longer than Ryker's. Feeling the crowbar transform in my hands into something, I open my eyes... And see a wooden mallet.

"What the hell is wrong with me?" I yell, hurling the thing at the wall. "I don't know what to do anymore. This thing is incorrigible."

"Pick it up." Ryker stares at me, still holding out his sword.

I pick it up and try again, and again, and again, but the damn thing takes on every shape imaginable... Except a sword.

After an hour of fighting with it, I'm at my wit's end. I'm exhausted and frustrated to tears. Ryker moves closer, holding out his sword. There's nothing I can do. I've done everything, and nothing worked.

When I don't move, he grabs me, spins me around, and holds my back against his chest, the flat side of his blade pressed to my throat, the killing edge skimming along the bottom of my chin. "Fight or die," he growls. "Your choice."

I'm out of breath, and I'm glad to feel that he is, too. His chest heaves against my back with each breath. His body is damp with sweat under the white shirt and tie he wears, like all the students. The heady, fresh scent of his sweat makes my head swim, and suddenly, all I can think about is his hot, hard body pressing against mine. My spork is beyond useless, but I have one weapon I haven't used.

Ignoring the blade at my throat, I melt back against Ryker, pushing my backside gently against his dress slacks, letting him feel the roundness of my ass moving against his crotch. I close my eyes and press back harder, grinding against him. Mere moments pass before I can feel his erection throbbing against me. A shudder of longing wracks my body, and I have to fight the urge to reach back and grab the huge, hard cock crushed to my ass.

Ryker's sword clatters to the floor. A low growl reverberates through his chest, vibrating my back and making me hot all over. I squirm against him, wanting more. He grasps my chin and turns my face around, angling his mouth to mine. I respond hungrily, without thought. I know this guy is an asshole who just drove me to tears, but I don't care. My body doesn't care. It only wants one thing—him.

I want his sweating body riding mine, his thick cock pounding into me endlessly, his cum filling me to overflowing. The dirtiness of my thoughts shocks me, but it also makes me even hotter. Wet heat throbs between my legs, and I moan into his mouth.

Term 1: Unleashing Trials

He lifts my chin, his kiss increasing in pressure and intensity. My breath comes heavy and fast as I arch back against him, needing more, and he gives it. I gasp, and his tongue slides inside. He lets out a helpless groan, and pleasure ripples through me and slides between my thighs. I can feel the heat and wetness there increasing as his tongue caresses mine, slowly at first and then faster, thrusting into my mouth. His hands explore my body, pressing over my ribs, cupping my breasts, pinching at my nipples through the fabric of my uniform. His other hand slides down my belly and under my skirt, fingering my soaked panties. He groans again, rolling his hips against mine.

"Ryker," I breathe, tingles exploding in places I didn't know existed. "Fuck, I want you."

As if I've flipped a switch, Ryker leaps away from me. He stares at me, turbulent emotions swirling over his features, and then his face settles into an inscrutable expression.

Then he laughs. *Laughs.*

If this is his attempt at throwing me off my game while keeping his own dignity, it works.

I'm mortified.

"I'll remember how easy you are next time I need to get laid," he says, swiping his sword off the floor, striding across the room, and disappearing out the door.

I stand there a second, too humiliated and pissed to move. What was I thinking? These guys are all the same. Zebras don't change their stripes, and assholes don't become nice guys.

Well, fuck him. Fuck all of them.

Shaking my head, I pick up my spork, stuff it into my pocket, and head to my room to change my ruined skirt and wet panties. I don't even care what time it is or what class I have next. I'm not about to show up looking flushed and disheveled, giving the Bellas more ammunition than they already have.

The first half of my walk is fast, but it's such a nice day today—not too humid, not too hot—I decide after that disappointment, I need to cheer up. May as well enjoy the weather on my way back. I even decide to take the long way, walking behind the academy along the edge of the woods.

The closer I get to the dorms, however, the weirder I start to feel. Like there's something following me. Occasionally, I glance behind me when I hear leaves rustling or something in the bushes, but there's nothing behind me.

Still, it gives me a creeped out feeling, and I pick up the pace. After the second attack by that disappearing hot lady, I know I'm not entirely safe off campus, but the Academy of Sorcery is protected by heavy magical spells and safeguards. No one can even get onto campus without being invited by a resident, which means a student would have to be following me. If one is, they're wearing an invisibility spell.

Right before I clear the back of the building, I hear a rustling in a nearby saw palmetto. I grab my spork and pray it's done being pissed at me. Suddenly, a hissing demonling leaps from the bush and lands on the path behind me in a crouch.

"Fucking A," I mutter to myself. The demonling is small and horned, with greyish skin and beady black eyes filled with malice. I don't know much about demonlings, but I know that despite their size, they're incredibly fierce. And I know this one's about to attack me. Clutching my spork, I imagine that it's a sword.

My spork turns into a cane just as the demonling lunges for me. It's less than half my height but incredibly compact, and it hits me like a ton of bricks. I stumble backwards, smacking it with my cane. The thing retreats, baring a row of shark-like teeth as it hisses louder.

Shit. I swing for it with my cane, but it leaps aside with surprising nimbleness considering its stout stature.

"What do you want?" I shout, swiping at it again.

It charges at me in response. Not that I expected an answer. Demonlings are pretty limited when it comes to speech.

"Go away," I yell.

But it doesn't go away. It ducks under my cane as it arcs toward the little beast. The next second, a fifty-pound weight slams into my legs, knocking me to the ground. Fear shoots through me, and I try to jump up, but the demonling clings to my legs, pinning me to the ground.

I'm beating it over the head with my cane, cursing the damn spork with the fury of a woman about to die, when footsteps sound on the path. The next second, Ryker appears over us.

The demonling looks over its shoulder, then leaps at my throat.

I scream.

Ryker's sword blurs through the air, and the demon's head topples to the ground beside me.

Fighting back another scream, I roll over as quickly as I can, dumping the body and scrambling away from it as I jump to my feet. "Are you hurt?" Ryker asks, reaching over to help brush me off.

"What the hell just happened?" I ask.

"You were attacked by a demon," Ryker points out. "A minor one, but still a demon."

"I know what it was," I say through clenched teeth.

"You do?" he asks, looking a bit surprised.

I'm well acquainted with the magical community, but it strikes me that he's telling me because he thinks I don't know. Not to be an ass. A lot of the kids here are privileged because their families use magic to get ahead. They went to the same preppy high school and hung out with each other on weekends. I might actually have an advantage for once. While they were learning about history and conjugating verbs, I was working for Silas, who was quite involved with the entire supernatural community, not just magic wielders. I decide to keep that to myself for now.

"There shouldn't be any demons on campus," Ryker says, frowning at the body on the ground. "It's supposed to be sealed off from outsiders."

"I think it was here for me," I admit.

Instead of scoffing and telling me I'm full of myself, Ryker eyes my bare legs. "Undoubtedly," he says. "But even on campus, you're not supposed to be alone. That's why you have guards."

"I seem to remember my 'guard' walking out on me a few minutes ago."

Ryker gives me a sour look. "I thought you were going to your next class. You seemed pretty worried about missing Professor Darius."

Do I detect a note of... Jealousy?

"I couldn't exactly go to class in this," I say, gesturing to my half-skirt. "Or maybe I could..."

Ryker takes my elbow in his hand and marches me toward the dorm. He is totally jealous.

The thought gives me more pleasure than it should. It was just a kiss. One that was totally and completely calculated and meant to distract him from murdering me. That's it. It had nothing to do with any actual attraction between us.

Who am I kidding? When I look up at him, it's all I can do not to drool. His sculpted jawline, even the golden bristle of his stubble, makes me sigh. His eyes, when they're not boring into me with hatred, are a storm I want to chase. And I can still feel his hard chest and abs against my back, the even harder ridge of his erection aching to push inside me. The thought sends a tremor straight to my core, and heat pools between my legs again.

"You're staring," Ryker says, not looking at me.

I turn away, trying not to blush.

Okay, fine, I'm attracted to him. But that is not the distraction I need right now. I was just attacked, for fuck's sake. I try to think of all I know about demonlings. Unlike regular demons, these guys aren't smart or cunning. They're viscous little monsters that do the grunt work for men like Silas. He "employed" a few, though I rarely saw them. While I scrubbed toilets, they did the more questionable dirty work he needed done—like disposing of bodies.

My mind immediately goes to my boss. Demonlings don't normally attack people without provocation or pay, and if they do, it's because of a perceived wrong the person did. Since I've never actually met a demonling, I couldn't have offended one. Which means someone sent this one after me.

And I know someone who has them at his disposal, someone who's not too happy with me. The only thing I don't know is what he hopes to gain by killing me.

Chapter 11

After class a few days later, I'm halfway to the dorm when I'm distracted by the sight of Elowen walking ahead of us, her head down as she shuffles along the sidewalk.

I haven't seen her in a week, and she doesn't look so good. I start toward her without thinking, waving and calling her name.

"That's a dark magic student," Thorn says, taking my arm. "You can't trust her. She could have summoned that demonling in one of her classes."

Because of course he knows about that. I can only hope Ryker didn't tell him the other thing that happened on Monday. The thing I will never think of again.

"*You're* a dark magic student," I remind him, pulling my arm away.

Thorn frowns, his green eyes darkening. "I can control my magic."

"Elowen is not evil," I say, squaring my shoulders. "She's my friend. You can boss me around all you want, but you can't tell me who to be friends with."

I glare up at him, but he shows no sign of emotion. In fact, he's shown me nothing but a poker face since the visit to my dad. He wouldn't even tell me about his injury, or if he's okay now. Mostly, he's just a big, silent, scowling oaf.

A freakishly sexy oaf who makes my heart do funny fluttering things inside my chest that cannot be healthy. I should probably see the campus doctor about it.

Turning away from him, I jog to catch up with Elowen. Thorn makes no move to stop me, but he follows a few paces behind like my own personal bodyguard.

"Hey, what's up?" I ask when I join Elowen.

"Nothing," she says with a sigh.

"Come on, you're my friend," I say. "You can talk to me."

"It's silly," she says. "In high school, I was never invited to parties, anyway. I just thought when I came here…" She glances at Thorn and whispers, "Things might be different."

"You didn't get invited to a party?" I clarify.

She sighs again. "I told you it was silly."

"It's not silly," I assure her. I'm no stranger to being excluded from things. I missed out on lots of things when I dropped out of school, and even more when I had to turn down invitations because I was working. Eventually, my friends stopped asking me to do stuff altogether, and I lost touch with them. I remember how much it hurt.

"You can go," Elowen says, brightening a little. "It's tradition. It's this big bash they throw after the students survive their first month of school. It's always thrown by one of the seniors to welcome the new class."

"You're the new class," I point out.

"I'm in the House of Necromancy," she says. "We're not invited."

"Fuck that," I say. "There's nothing wrong with your magic."

I stew all the way back to the dorm. When we stop in front of it, Elowen gives me a searching look. "What are you thinking?"

"I'm thinking that if I'm invited, you can go as my guest."

"Really? You don't think they'll be mad?"

"I don't give a fuck if they are," I say, a smile finding my face. "You're just as good as anyone here. If you want to go, you're invited."

"Did you get an invitation?"

"No," I admit. "You know what that means, don't you?"

She shakes her head, nervously biting at a hangnail.

"It means we have a party to crash."

Chapter 12

"Well, look at you." Asher grabs my hands and holds them out, surveying my little black dress. It might be simple, but it fits me to a T. The unadorned, stretchy fabric hugs my curves like it was tailored just for me, though I found it in the closet, tags still attached. It might not be flashy, but it doesn't need to be. It accentuates my cleavage and highlights my small waist and long legs in all the right places. In this dress, I don't need flashy. I don't even need accessories. For the first time in maybe my entire life, I feel sexy as hell.

"Damn girl," Asher says. "Our resident sex goddess has risen."

"Stop calling me that," I say, but I can't help but laugh even as I roll my eyes. "Sex goddess, my ass. But you. Shit, Ash. You look hot." I grab his hand and drag him inside my room. He's wearing a pair of black skinny pants and a silvery silk shirt open at the neck to show a triangle of smooth ivory skin.

"Don't I?" he asks, striking a pose. Then he spots Elowen and rushes over to her, grabs her hands, and spins her in a circle. "Girl, you look amazing, too. Ready to party?"

She smiles, her cheeks going pink. "I guess."

For the past week, we've been plotting this nearly every day. Mostly Asher and I, since Elowen doesn't share any classes or even a dorm with us, but we tried to keep her in the loop.

"I can't believe we've survived a whole month at the Academy," Asher says. "It seems like we just got here."

It does, but at the same time, I've gotten used to life here. The nice room, the plentiful food, the classes, my friends. The one thing I'll never get used to is being followed around 24/7, but even that isn't always bad. Thorn and Ryker are mostly content to follow me in silence, and Rocco... Well, he's grown on me a bit. I sometimes even enjoy our little quibbles.

"Okay, let's do this," I say, grabbing my purse. "Do you guys know where we're going?"

"It's a few blocks off campus at Gideon's Bar," Asher says.

"Gideon's?" Elowen asks, her eyes widening and her cheeks flaming.

"Looks like there's somebody I need to meet," I tease, giving her a wink.

"It's not like that," she says quickly, but Asher rolls his eyes at me to show me otherwise.

"The doorman," Asher whispers theatrically.

"Okay, then," I say. "This should be fun. Let's go show those assholes what we're made of."

I fling open the door, ready to conquer the world.

And run smack into Rocco, who stands there wearing dark jeans slung low on his hips and a black T-shirt stretched across his broad, muscular shoulders. *Day-um* he looks good out of uniform.

"Please tell me you're not here to stop me from going to this party."

"Nope," he says, a twinkle of mischief in his eye.

"Or going to the party with us," I say, the sinking feeling in my belly growing worse as I take in his appearance. His blond hair is combed back, the golden strands gleaming under the lights like they're wet. And he smells fresh and soapy, and those jeans are really nice, and…

"I'm afraid so," he says, twirling a keyring around his finger and grinning at me.

"Ugh, why?" I groan, smacking my forehead with my palm.

"Assuming that's not a rhetorical question, the answer is simple," he says. "Cinderella needs an escort to the ball, and it's my turn."

"Your turn to ruin all fun?" I ask. "Super. I had so much fun with your brothers Kill Joy and Spoil Sport when it was their turn."

Rocco throws back his head and laughs. It strikes me that I've never heard him laugh before—not a real laugh. The sound is deep and rolling, so joyous that I can't help but smile despite myself.

The four of us take off toward the bar, which is only a few blocks from campus. I've heard of Gideon's—it's the only supernaturals-only bar in Jacksonville—but I've never been.

"I don't need a chaperone," I say to Rocco as we walk. "I won't be alone. I'll have Asher and Elowen and a whole bar full of people around me the whole time."

I glance back over my shoulder at Asher, who flashes me an encouraging thumbs-up.

"Oh, did you think I was worried about you?" Rocco asks, motioning to his chest. "No, you misunderstand. I just want to be there to watch you make a fool of yourself."

I glare at him. "What makes you think you'll get to see that?"

"Because I'm your guard tonight," he says, as if it's obvious.

"You seriously think I can't go a single night without making a fool of myself?"

"Oh, I don't think it, Cinderella," he says. "I know it."

"We'll see, Pumpkin."

Rocco smiles and appraises me from the corner of his eye. "Okay, I'll bite. Why *Pumpkin?*"

"Well, you called me Cinderella, and you said you were my escort to the ball. Pretty sure the pumpkin is Cinderella's escort. Plus, you know, your head kinda looks like a pumpkin. That toothy grin."

I give him a toothy grin to demonstrate, and again, he laughs. Damn it. I wish his laugh weren't quite so infectious.

"Pumpkin," he says. "Huh. I like it. Though I think a jack-o-lantern has a few less teeth than me."

"That can be arranged," I say, holding up my fists.

"You know, you're not so bad when you're not being a total brat," he says. "You should try it more often."

"Right back at you."

We arrive at Gideon's, only to see a line of students with invitations clutched in their hands waiting to get in. The Bellas are at the front, flipping their shiny hair and flirting with the doorman, a blond guy leaning against the wall looking like jeans were invented just for him.

"So that's the reason you were all aflutter when I mentioned Gideon's," I say to Elowen, elbowing her gently.

"It doesn't matter," she says, going pink to the roots of her brown hair. "He'd never even look at me. He could have the Bellas if he wanted them."

"Well, if he's worth your time, he wouldn't want them," I say.

He finally takes the invites from the Bellas, and they sashay inside and disappear.

"Shit," I say. "We need one of those?"

"'Fraid so," Rocco says, hooking his thumbs in his front pockets and watching us with an amused expression.

"I hear they rent out the entire club for the night," Asher says, his words quick with excitement. "It's only open for academy students during the back-to-school bash."

"Well, this academy student didn't get an invite," I say.

"I got one," he says, looking guilty. "But I won't go in without y'all."

"And why wasn't I invited?" I ask.

"Because you're supposed to be safe on campus in your dorm," Rocco reminds me.

"How will we get in?" Elowen asks, wringing her hands. "They won't let us in the front door."

"Then we'll sneak in the back." I nod to a wide, empty alleyway beside the building. We traipse down it to the single metal door set into the brick. Unfortunately, it's locked.

"How you gonna get in now, Houdini?" Rocco asks, looking more amused by the second.

"Like this." I pull out my spork, close my eyes and imagine it a key. For once, she does what I want, and the next second, I slip the key into the lock. I raise my eyebrows at Rocco. "You were saying?"

"Well played," he says, holding up both hands. I open the door and step inside, my friends close behind. We descend a flight of stairs and move through a storage room, hurrying toward a doorway into what looks like a bar. As we round the end of a stack of beer boxes, a guy in a chair jumps to his feet, scaring the shit out of all of us.

"What are you doing here?" he asks, looking as freaked out as the rest of us. He's got long, snow-white hair that hangs in sheets to nearly his waist, and his skin is pearly white with a glimmering sheen.

"Oh my god, you nearly gave us a heart attack," Asher says, covering his heart. "We just stepped outside to smoke."

"That door should be locked," the pale guy says. "Why isn't it locked?"

Asher shrugs. "No idea, man."

"Are you Gideon?" I ask, holding out a hand. "Jade. Nice to meet you."

"Oh, no, I'm… Bob." The hesitation makes it clear he just made that up on the fly.

"Bob," Rocco says, his eyes narrowing.

"Yep," the guy says. "Bob. I'm, uh, an albino." He's clearly not human, but I have no idea what he is. I've never seen anyone like him. His eyes are gold and sparkling. Not gold like a cat, but gold like a freaking pile of glitter.

"I see that," Asher says, looking way too interested. We need to get out of here before a bouncer comes and tosses us out.

"Yep," Bob says again. "Albino Bob. That's me."

"Well, it's nice to meet you, Albino Bob," I say. "I don't mean to be rude, but we'd better go find our friends."

If he has reasons for not telling us his real name, that's his business. As long as he's not going to throw us out, I don't care what his name is.

"Oh, um, I'm afraid I better get Gideon if that door is open," he says.

"Oh, no," Rocco says in a mock horrified tone, a smile on his face as he watches us fail at our party crashing attempt. His gloating grin is just what I need to get me going.

"I don't think that's a good idea," I say. "I mean, sure, do that, but let's just wait until we're out on the dance floor. Otherwise, we'll have to stand in line, and we'll probably get to talking to all those students waiting to get in. I'm sure they'll

167

want to know all about the really cool albino guy we met in the back room."

Bob's glittering gold eyes focus on mine, and I can't help but stare at the shifting light in them. Suddenly, I feel a little lightheaded. I yank my eyes away from his, my heart thudding. Fuck. He's got some kind of hypnotic power.

"Go to the party," he says after a slight hesitation. "And don't cause any trouble."

"No trouble," I say, grabbing Asher's arm and dragging him away before he can fall under Bob's weird hypnosis.

"What was that?" Elowen asks with a shudder, glancing over her shoulder as we dart out the door and into the bar. "Fae?"

"No idea, but we're in now," I say. "That's the important part."

Music is blaring, and the small dance floor is already filling. The club is a rectangular space with pool tables, a bar along one wall, and tables and chairs along another. But the main attraction is clearly the dance floor complete with DJ booth.

The three of us head in that direction. I'm excited to blend in with the rest of the students enjoying a night out. I let the beat guide me, moving to the rhythm with Asher and Elowen beside me. This is honestly the first time I've ever done something like this. Closing my eyes, I let go. Song after song, I dance to the music, moving my body, enjoying a little taste of freedom.

After a while, I feel a pair of warm hands sliding around my waist. I turn, expecting to see Asher, or maybe a guy I'll need to blow off. But it's Rocco. I'm not sure what to do. I didn't expect him to join the party, but now that I think about it, of course he is. Guys like him are the reason these kinds of parties exist.

He smiles down at me, the dimple sinking into his cheek, and for once he doesn't say a word. His hands guide my hips, helping me find my rhythm after the interruption. I think about resisting, but then decide not to. If he's not going to drag me off the dance floor and stop me from having a good time, I'm okay with him. He's no longer an enemy, despite his occasional rudeness and coarse words. And it's nice to have a partner after dancing solo for a while.

I shimmy to the music, grinning at Asher who dances in front of me. He mouths, "Oh my god," and fans himself, presumably when Rocco isn't looking. After a couple songs, Rocco's grip on my hips tightens, and he pulls me flush against him. The full-body contact sends a wave of heat through me, and I begin to move my hips in a more sultry rhythm. I slowly grind against him, breathless as the friction between our bodies builds. I can feel his rigid cock straining against the softness of my ass, and my desire flares higher. I lay my head back against his chest, reveling in the sensations of all his huge, hard muscles against my soft body.

When I open my eyes, I have the sensation of being watched. I glance around, and my gaze connects with Thorn's. He's sitting on a stool at the bar, but he's turned to the dance floor, openly staring. The hunger in his eyes sends a chill straight through me to my core, and my clit throbs in response. If the enormous tent in the front of his pants is any indication, the feeling is completely mutual. Without thinking, I make a beckoning gesture.

I blink, and he's gone. Shit. Of course uptight Thorn doesn't dance. Besides that, I'm already dancing with his friend.

I close my eyes, telling myself it doesn't matter if he dances with me. I have Rocco, who is more than enough, judging from the huge cock he's got shoved against my ass. I start grinding on him even harder, trying to forget the sting of rejection. And then I feel another pair of hands on my hips. My eyes fly open, and I find Thorn in front of me, his eyes blazing with heat. He tightens his grip, and his thigh parts mine and slides between.

My breath catches as I wait for Rocco to chase him off, to tell Thorn that I already have a partner. But he only rolls his hips against mine, pushing my body against Thorn's. A gasp escapes me when I feel both their cocks, rigid and ready, grinding into me at once. Excitement races through me, and wetness springs to life between my legs. I move between them, imagining a very different scene involving a bedroom and a lot less clothes between the three of us.

I don't think I've ever had such a naughty fantasy, and my desire throbs inside me with the rhythm of the music, making me so wet I can feel slickness soaking my panties and coating my thighs. Thorn's hands slide behind me, grabbing my ass and pulling me tighter against him. I don't know if it's the intended effect, but he parts my ass cheeks, and the length of Rocco's cock settles between. At the same time, Thorn's thigh muscle is flexing to the beat, pumping against my swollen clit with each movement.

I loop one arm around Rocco's neck behind me, and one around Thorn's. Our eyes stay locked together, and he grinds slowly against me, gripping my ass while Rocco grips my thighs from behind, spreading them for Thorn. Thorn pivots to the center, positioning himself against me, and suddenly, it's not his thigh grinding against my clit. The heat and hardness of his erection crushes against me, and before I know what's happening, a wave of pleasure grips my body. My hands tighten on both men, fisting in their hair, as helpless pleasure washes over me. My knees give way, but they support me, their cocks throbbing against me as my core clenches again and again.

Chapter 13

Before I've even recovered or absorbed the fact that I just had my first non-magical orgasm, and it was in the middle of a dance floor while sandwiched between two men who I'm not even sure I like, someone grabs Rocco and yanks him back. I expect to see Ryker behind him, but it's someone I don't even know. Rocco tries to push him off, but another guy steps in, trying to get behind me. Someone else grabs my elbow, trying to drag me away from Thorn, who throws a punch at the guy.

Suddenly, fists are flying, and people are grabbing me from every side, trying to drag me away. I throw punches along with the rest of them. Anyone who grabs me gets knocked out by my mean left hook. Girls shriek and try to scramble away, and a guy tromps right over another guy on the floor, diving for me.

"What's happening?" I yell, but everyone is too busy fighting to answer. A pair of hands grabs me from behind, and I turn and slam my fist into his jaw.

"What the fuck?" Ryker asks, grabbing my hands and restraining them.

"Sorry," I yell. "Touch me, and you get punched."

"What the hell are you doing here, Jade?" he growls. "You weren't invited—for a reason."

A guy dives at us, but Ryker pivots, blocking me with his body. He throws an elbow, and the guy goes down.

"Excluding me for my magic is just as shitty as excluding the dark magic students for theirs," I yell at Ryker. "What magic we have is not a choice. We didn't do anything wrong."

He gives me a look that says I'm full of shit.

"Fine, maybe I have, but Elowen didn't," I say. "Either invite everyone, or don't have the party in the first place."

Someone grabs me, and my hands are wrenched free of Ryker's. I fall to the floor with the guy, and Ryker dives onto us, wrestling the guy away. I roll away and jump to my feet, leaping aside when Ryker and the other guy roll toward me.

Suddenly, everything stops. The music stops, leaving only an echo. The voices stop, leaving their echo along with the music. And everyone freezes. Bodies are contorted into fighting pairs and groups. Girls are huddled together in the corner, unmoving, unblinking. Rocco's fist is pulled back to deliver a punch that never came. Thorn and another guy are eternally choking each other. Ryker has his attacker pinned to the floor, frozen.

A soft scuffing sound echoes through the room as someone moves. I spin around, terror ricocheting through my brain. The room is so shadowy, filled with statues. I can't tell who moved.

"Who's there?" I demand, my voice sounding as panicked as I feel.

A man steps from between two others, and my heart nearly explodes with fear. I don't know this guy, and he seems to be the only person in the bar still alive. And I'm alone with him— the one thing I've been warned against.

His posture is tense but not threatening. Almost the opposite. He looks wary, ready for any sudden movement. Is he waiting for me to run? He's not particularly... Well, anything. He's not huge like my sorcerer guards, but he's tall. He has dark hair, not black like Thorn's, but a deep chestnut color. He's thirtyish, handsome but not remarkably. The important details aren't his looks, though. What matters is that I have no protection, and if he froze all these people, or froze time, he must be unimaginably powerful.

And me? I don't even have my uncooperative gag-gift utensil. It's in my purse, which is at a table across the bar where a statue of Elowen sits with a drink halfway to her mouth. I'm unarmed, untrained, and trapped.

"What the fuck just happened?" I ask, backing toward the tables, my mind racing. "Did you do this?"

"Not entirely," he says. "I don't allow brawling in my bar."

"You're Gideon."

He nods, his face entirely blank, even more so than my guards, who might put on a blank face, but I can tell there's something under their expressions. He's not tense like they are, just relaxed and serene and frighteningly calm. I can tell when they're trying not to show their hand. I have no idea what this guy wants, no idea what he's thinking.

"Your ride is waiting," he says, gesturing to the bar. "You need to leave. This won't last forever."

"My friends—"

"Are fine," he interrupts. He gives a firm nod toward the back door, and I edge that way, trying not to look too closely at the deathly still figures around me. The bartender stands pouring a drink, the liquid frozen in midair.

Holy shit. Did Gideon just freeze the world? He said it wasn't exactly what I thought. Maybe it's an illusion. Whatever he did, it's scary as hell. I grab my purse and obey, figuring if he wanted to murder me, he'd have done it already. I scurry through the storage room through which we entered—no sign of Albino Bob this time—up the stairs, and out the back door.

Professor Darius stands outside the door, bouncing on his toes and glancing around as if he expects an ambush.

"Come on," he says, taking my arm and steering me out the back of the alley, where a familiar black town car sits idling. He opens the door and hurries me in, closing the door behind me before circling the car and sliding into the driver's seat. He glances in the rearview mirror and then makes his way through the dimly lit parking lot.

"What are you doing here?" I ask at last, feeling like a kid who got caught doing something wrong. Which I suppose I am, but I don't want him thinking of me like a kid in need of a lecture. Even if he's a teacher, and nothing can ever happen between us, he's a hot teacher. Some part of me wants him to admire me, if not as much as I admire him, at least a fraction of that.

"Ryker told me I might find you here," he says.

The bastard.

"It's not safe for you to be here, Jade. You must know that by now."

"I do," I say. "But isn't that why I have guards? So I can be a normal student and do what they do? So why can't I go out and dance like any other girl?"

"In an ideal world, that would be the case," Darius says with a sigh. "I'm sorry, Jade. You're not just another girl."

The way he says those words makes my heart dance. It's far better than seeing him admire me physically. "Okay," I say, looking out the window to hide my smile.

"I'll make sure there's more for you to do on campus in the future. I hadn't realized how much you wanted to fit in with your peers."

My peers. No, no, no. Now he's lumping me in with everyone else, after telling me I was special. Like he thinks I don't want to be special, don't want my magic. Like he thinks I'd rather be normal than a girl who makes him say things like he just said.

"Maybe next time, you can entertain me," I say lightly, watching his reaction from the corner of my eye.

He swallows and adjusts his hands on the steering wheel. "I know this must be frustrating," he says. "I don't think you quite realize the effect you have on men. All men, Jade. Including the three who have been charged with guarding you."

"And you?" I sneak a peek at him, my heart hammering as I wait for his response.

Finally, after the longest minute of silence of my life, Darius clears his throat. "You're a student," he says, pulling into the parking lot of the campus, behind the dorm.

We sit in the car for a minute, silent.

"I am sorry," he says. "But you saw what happened tonight. Until you've really mastered your magic, it's better to stay on campus where we can look after you." He opens the door and gets out, then opens my door from the outside.

"That's what happened?" I ask, stepping out of the car. I feel suddenly awkward as hell. Did my sex magic get loose when I got aroused? I knew my magic was unwieldy, but shit. I didn't mean to incite a riot.

"From what I heard, yes."

"When?" I ask. Because all I can think about is how Rocco danced with me without making a single shitty comment, and how stoic Thorn got up and rubbed all up on me. And how they didn't seem to even care that I was dancing with both of them. Was all that the magic, and not me? The thought somehow hurts, as if my magic betrayed me. In a way, it did. I didn't know I was releasing it. I thought, for a second, that it was me. That they wanted me.

"I can't know that," Darius says gently. "I wasn't there."

"Well, that explains it," I say, turning toward the dorm.

Professor Darius escorts me inside the dorm, which is quiet and deserted. Everyone is still at the party, welcoming the freshmen. "What does it explain?" my teacher asks as we start up the stone steps.

"Nothing," I say. "Just why the sorcerers forgot they hated me for five minutes."

"Jade," he says.

The sympathy in his voice makes my throat tighten painfully. I don't want his kindness. It'll break me faster than all the cruelty the others have dished out all year.

"Professor Darius," I say, stopping to face him at the door to my room.

He rubs his temple. "Your guards don't hate you," he says. "They're trying their best to keep a professional distance, the same way I am. It must be hard for them to be around you so much. If they're being too harsh, I'll speak to them."

"No, it's fine." I can just imagine the hell my life will be if I rat them out. "They're not," I insist. "I can handle it."

He gives a small smile. "I'm sure you can. You've dealt with a lot. More than someone your age should have to deal with."

My age. I wince at the words. He might as well be broadcasting it over the loudspeakers: *Never gonna happen.*

We linger in the hallway, not awkward but... Expectant. As if we're both waiting for the other to say the magic words.

"Do you..." I break off, swallowing hard. "Do you want to come in?"

"Oh, I—I can't." He shakes his head. "That wouldn't be..."

"Of course," I say.

"I'll be out here tonight," he says. "Guess I should see what it's like."

I swallow, my pulse fluttering in my throat. Is he having trouble keeping a professional distance, too?

"Thanks for coming to get me, Professor Darius," I say, squeezing his forearm.

"Darius is fine," he says. Our gazes lock, linger, and my heartbeat thrums in my ears.

"Goodnight, Darius," I say, feeling shy suddenly. I pull back from my touch, and he links his hands behind his back and steps across the hall, leaning against the wall.

"Goodnight, Jade."

I lie in bed for a long time before sleep comes. Thinking about the professor outside my door. Wondering if he's thinking about me. Thinking about the three men who have treated me badly, maybe only to keep from getting too close. And wondering if they're thinking about me, too. Eventually, I hear other students returning from the party. I try not to think about the fact that my guards don't return to my door that night. I try not to care where they are.

Chapter 14

On the way to my first class, the absurdly early swordsmanship class that kicks my ass every morning, Asher nudges my shoulder and grins. "So, I hear you left with the professor last night. Hot."

My cheeks turn red as I bump him back. "Stop."

"Seriously, though," Asher says. "What's it like having all those guys all over you? Was it awesome or what?"

I narrow my eyes. "You mean when they started brawling because a little of my magic leaked out? Yeah, that was *awesome.*"

"Called it," says a voice from behind us.

I roll my eyes toward Asher. "Called what?" I yell back over my shoulder.

"The whole 'making an ass of yourself' thing," Rocco says, jogging up behind us.

"If I recall, you weren't exactly keeping your cool, either," I shoot back.

Asher snickers, then covers his mouth trying to hide it.

"Next time put a little more of your genie in the bottle, Cinderella," Rocco says with a grin. "You're giving us all blue balls."

"You have a hand," I say, wiggling my fingers at him.

"I bet it's even worse for you," Rocco says. "I mean, you've got the magic."

"I have no idea what you're talking about," I say, though he's not kidding when he says it's gotta be hard for me. Lately, I've been just about ready to jump his bones, and I hate him. Sort of, anyway.

"You know, I could help you release some of that tension," Rocco says. "I'm not picky."

"Ouch," Asher mutters.

"Wow, I feel so special," I say, rolling my eyes. "Does that line actually work for you?"

"I don't need pickup lines," Rocco says, crossing his thick arms over his bulging pectorals, flexing them a little for my enjoyment.

"I need brains along with the beauty," I say.

Asher veers off to go to his weapons class, where he's mastering his nunchucks, while I continue on toward Ryker's class.

"You know, you can keep being a tease if that's your thing," Rocco says with a shrug. "It's definitely teaching us a lesson in self-control."

"Excuse me?" I ask, glaring daggers at him. "I'm no tease. I can't help what magic I have."

"You can help what you do with it."

I start to protest, then remember I said exactly the same thing to Elowen. Is he right? I mean, I definitely wasn't complaining when he and Thorn were rubbing up against me last night. In fact, I called Thorn over to join us. I wasn't trying to be a tease. I was just having fun dancing. But now that he's said it, I can see how it came across that way, especially since I never had any intention of letting it go further than dancing. The sting of what Professor Darius said last night comes back to me. It was my magic attracting them, not me. Now it feels even worse than rejection. It feels like I did something gross, enchanting them against their will.

"I'm sorry," I say at last. "I just wanted to dance like everyone else. I wasn't thinking about my magic. I'll try to be more responsible."

For once, Rocco looks utterly speechless.

If I've managed a truce, it does not extend to his brother. When I arrive at swordsmanship class, Ryker immediately claims me for a demonstration and drags me to the front of the class.

I step up slowly, humiliation already building inside me. The class is small, since only those with various types of swords practice here. But embarrassing myself in front of ten other students still sucks.

"Ready your sword," Ryker says.

I sigh and hold up my spork.

"I'm an attacker. I'm going to hurt you if you can't control your weapon," he growls. "Do it."

I close my eyes and focus as hard as I can, picturing a sword. And also wishing Professor Darius taught this class, since he wouldn't do this to me.

A ripple of laughter goes through the students, and I open my eyes. I'm holding a butter knife.

"Hey, it's a start," I say, brandishing it with a grin. "I mean, it's more sword-like than a spork."

A couple people laugh, which is better than them making fun of me. I bow dramatically, then hold up my kitchen knife. "Ladies and gentleman, I give you… Excalibur."

Ryker snatches the knife from my hand, and the giggles immediately cease.

"You think this is funny?" Ryker asks, towering over me. "If this were really happening, you'd be dead right now."

"Don't touch my spork," I growl, snatching it back.

Ryker steps closer, his eyes burning with anger. "Then stop fucking around. You're wasting everyone's time."

"Me? What about her?" I ask, brandishing the silly knife, who I've started to think of as female. A stubborn bitch, to be more exact.

"Do you want your magic to control you for the rest of your life?" Ryker asks, his eyes burning into mine. "You own your magic, not the other way around."

"Yeah, well, she's not cooperating, as you can see," I say, stuffing the knife into my waistband and planting my hands on my hips. "So how about *you* stop wasting my time? You could have given me a real sword to practice with all this time so I could learn something. Or hell, give me a wooden dummy sword to spar with instead of teaching everyone else while I stand around yelling at a stupid spork."

"Take control of your weapon," Ryker says, his voice menacing as he raises his sword, pressing the tip of it to my chest.

My face burning with rage, I yank out the kitchen knife and glare down at it, hating him and my stupid magic and this fucking spork with all my energy. It squirms in my hand, and the next second, a shoelace dangles from my hand.

The class laughs.

Ryker drops his sword and grabs me by the throat. "Get out of my class," he growls through clenched teeth. "Don't come back until you can take this seriously."

I jerk away, balling the shoelace in my hand. "Fine," I say. "This class is a waste of my time, anyway."

"You're a waste of my time, Jade," Ryker says quietly.

My eyes burning with tears, I turn and run out of the class. My footsteps echo down the hall as I run to the bathroom. I stand at the sink, splashing cold water over my hot face until my skin cools and my tears are washed away.

In my next class, I fall into my seat in a dispirited lump. I left halfway through my other class, which means no one else has arrived in Professor Darius's class. After the party, I'm not sure my intrusion is welcome, but if I go back to the dorm, I may never come out.

"Everything all right, Jade?" Professor Darius asks, stuffing his hands in his pockets and rocking up on his heels as he stands next to his desk.

"No," I groan, dropping my forehead to the surface of my desk. "I can't get my spork to cooperate at all. It refuses to turn into a sword again."

"But she did it before?"

"Yes, when I was about to die," I say.

"So, she showed up for you when you really needed her," he says. "Did you thank her?"

"Um… No. I'm not in the habit of talking to inanimate objects."

Darius smiles a little and moves toward my desk, stopping a few feet away like he doesn't want to get too close to me and my unpredictable magic. "She chose you," he says. "That's not something an inanimate object does. I know it can seem that way at times, but remember, your magic is alive."

"I know," I say, nodding. "And I've moved magic back and forth between me and her in your class. Because you're a good teacher. Ryker just yells at me and does his best to humiliate me in front of the class."

"Maybe he's trying to find something to motivate you," Darius says, halfway sitting on one of the nearby desks, one foot still on the floor. He clasps his hands on his knee, which makes my eyes wander from there up to the bulge in his pants. I gulp and tear my eyes away.

"I think he's trying to get me to leave the academy," I say.

"That's not really an option, though, is it?" Darius asks, cocking his head to one side.

"You could bind my magic forever, couldn't you? I've heard of that happening."

He shakes his head. "Maybe for a witch or wizard, but I don't think that can work for you. You were chosen as the High Priestess, Jade. You can't walk away from that magic, no matter how much it scares you."

It does scare me. I'm a freaking virgin. What do I know about being a sex goddess? But I haven't been sabotaging myself because of it.

At least, I don't think I have.

"Where's your weapon?" Darius asks gently.

I sigh and pull out the string, setting it on my desk. "Scary, huh?"

Instead of laughing, Darius nods. "What's her name?"

He did tell us during a class that we should name our weapon, that she's half of our team. I don't think Stubborn Bitch was what he had in mind.

"You're telling me to be nice to her, and Ryker is telling me to be mean," I say. "Which one is it?"

"I'm not telling you to be nice," Darius says. "I'm telling you to respect her. She holds your magic. But you're in control of it. Treat her with respect, as you respect your magic, but be firm with her. You're the wielder of that magic."

The gentleness in his voice makes me want to cry all over again, but I suck it up and focus on my weapon. What the hell do I name an uncooperative spork?

"So, if I name her, you're saying she'll cooperate?"

"I'm saying you have to build a relationship with her," he says. "Think of her more like… A dog. You're her owner. She will be obedient to you, but you have to train her to be. You have to let her know that you're her boss. She can tell if you're uncertain, if you're resentful. But she's also shown up for you when you truly needed her."

"You're right," I say. "She's loyal to me. I should be loyal to her."

"Why don't you start coming by in the afternoons, after your classes, to practice a little and catch up?" Professor Darius asks.

It's stupid how happy that makes me, considering we can't be together in any way beyond him teaching me. But I'm determined to make him proud of me, to make him think I'm worthy of my magic.

I try to think of a name all day, but I have no idea what to name a clairvoyant spork with discipline problems. I still haven't thought of one that night when I go to bed. Sometime after midnight, a tapping noise wakes me. For a second, I think someone must be at my door. But just as I throw off the blankets, I hear it again. It's not coming from the door. It's from the window.

I pull open the curtains to find Elowen on the fire escape, eyes red, cheeks stained with tears.

"What are you doing out here?" I whisper, opening the window to make room for her to wiggle through. I pick up my potted orchid, which I'd forgotten about and is now looking pretty grim, and set it on the desk next to the picture of my family so I don't forget it again. Elowen climbs in the window, and I close it behind her before turning on the light over the desk.

"What's wrong?"

"I can't be this way," she says, the words bursting from her. "If I keep going like this, I'll start doing evil things, and I don't want to. I can't go back to the House of Necromancy." She sits on my bed, pulls her knees to her chest, and starts sobbing uncontrollably.

"So don't," I say. "Don't go back. You can stay here. There's an extra bed, anyway."

Elowen looks up at me, her eyeliner smeared over her cheeks. "Won't we get in trouble?"

"We'll be fine," I say, smoothing her disheveled hair. "I've skipped lots of classes. And if you only leave here when I'm gone, my guards won't even see you. They leave when I leave. They'll never know."

She sniffs and lets out a shaky breath. "Thank you."

I dig in my drawers and toss her a T-shirt and a pair of sweats she can use and then turn down the bed as she changes into the clothes I gave her. Once I put out the light, we lie in bed in the dark. I can hear her breathing, which keeps me awake as I'm not used to sleeping in the same room as someone else.

"Are you awake?" I whisper after a while.

"Yeah," she says, sounding groggy.

"What would you name a bratty, psychic spork that contains all your magic?" I ask.

Elowen giggles, but it's not the mean laughter I usually hear when I refer to my weapon.

"Gus," she says.

I start laughing, too. "She's a girl. I'm thinking Cleo."

"I like it," she says. "What can you do with your magic, anyway?"

"Not much yet," I admit. "So far, mostly I just transfer it back and forth from Cleo." Saying the name, it sounds right.

"But what could you do with it?" Elowen presses. "Could you make someone fall in love with you?"

"I don't know," I say. "I'd never try something like that. It would be a total violation, not to mention pointless."

"How's it pointless?"

"Because they wouldn't really love me," I say. "It would just be the magic. I already have to worry about that enough with people being attracted to me, and that's not even love."

"Still," she says, shifting in her bed. "I wish someone was attracted to me."

"Elowen," I say. "I'm sure lots of guys are attracted to you."

She snorts in response.

"Listen, you're going to find someone who appreciates how kind you are despite your magic," I say. "Someone who loves and is attracted to you for just who you are. You don't need magic for that. You already have that kind of magic inside you."

"You really think so?"

"I know so."

She sniffs, then murmurs, "Thank you." Within minutes, she's sound asleep in my spare bed, and I drift off in mine.

Over the next few weeks, things start to even out. Elowen settles into my room, which is both challenging—I'm not used to having someone in my space every second I'm home—and amazing. I finally have a roommate like everyone else, and it's a lot less lonely being trapped in my room when I'm with someone else. Plus, sneaking around the sorcerers is kinda fun.

Between getting used to my new roommate and the added training on top of my regular classes, my next two weeks are full. As it turns out, Professor Darius is right. When I talk to Cleo, she finally begins to cooperate at least half the time, and I get to practice swordplay with the other students. In Darius's class, I practice the power exchange until I can move power back and forth between me and her as seamlessly as every other student. My extra sessions with Professor Darius definitely help, too—when I can keep myself from spending all my time staring at him and thinking of excuses to touch him, anyway.

Just when I'm starting to get the hang of working with Cleo, I arrive in class one day and can't find her in my bag.

"Get to work, Jade," Ryker demands as he strides around the room.

I empty out my backpack, desperately searching for my weapon. This time, it's completely different from when I threw her away. Now, a desperate, panicky feeling climbs my spine when I can't find her. I need her. I've gotten used to her, even when she's being a pain in the ass.

Ryker stops next to me. "Today, Jade."

"I don't have her."

"What do you mean?" Ryker asks, his eyes narrowing.

"She's not here," I repeat, keeping my voice low to minimize the staring, though I want to scream. "I put her in here yesterday after class. I know I did. I wouldn't lose her."

Ryker looks skeptical. I did throw her in the trash once, after all.

"You should have your weapon on you at all times," he says. "Go find it."

Throwing my bag back over my shoulder, I sprint across campus, back to the dorms. My heart is thundering in my ears. Even before I could use her, I didn't like other people touching Cleo. I have a connection with her that transcends her defiance and my frustration. She's mine. She's part of me, of my magic.

I tear my room apart, but the spork is nowhere to be found.

Fuckity Fuck. Where is she?

I look through all my stuff, even the drawers I gave Elowen, but it's nowhere. Trying not to completely lose my shit, I collapse onto the bed and run my fingers through my long, blonde locks, wracking my brain for any place I might have dropped my weapon. But I come up empty.

Chapter 15

Finally, I drag myself up and head out to see Professor Darius. But as soon as I step out the door, there's Rocco.

"Don't start with me today," I warn.

He surveys my messy hair, then glances back at the door to my room. "Lover's quarrel?"

"I wish," I mutter. If only it were that simple.

"What's up?" he asks as we start down the stairs.

I roll my eyes. "Are we sharing stuff now?"

"We could be."

I snort at that. "Right. Let me guess. I tell you something, and you use it against me and make fun of me for the rest of the year. Hmm, let me think."

"You know, I've been here three years, Jade. I have some of the strongest magic in the Academy. It's not beyond the realm of possibilities that I could help with whatever's bothering you." The look in his eyes is closer to plain exasperation than disdain now.

I decide to chance it. "I lost Cleo."

"Is that your spork, or the necromancy chick who's been living in your room for the past two weeks?"

"What?" I squeak. "There's no necromancy student living with me."

Rocco gives me a look. "Sharing, remember?"

"I shared," I say. "I lost Cleo. That's what's wrong."

"I bet you anything the necromancy chick took it."

"No way. She wouldn't do that."

He grins. "So, you admit she is living with you."

"I admit no such thing." I cross my arms and refuse to look at him as we cross the campus toward the main building. I knew he'd trick me somehow.

"You give her too much credit," he says. "She plays with life and death. She can't be trusted."

"That's bullshit," I say. "That's like saying I must be a slut because I have this... *Creative* magic."

"Sadly, I can attest to the fact that you are not a slut," he says. "The only action you've gotten since I've been here is with that chick, and it must suck, because you're both awfully quiet."

"I'm not sleeping with Elowen," I say. "Or anyone else, for that matter. Not that it's any of your business."

"You know, I could fix that," he says with a grin.

"No, thanks," I say. "When I have sex, it'll be with someone who doesn't call me Cinderella and treat me like a maid."

"You've never had sex, have you?"

"What? Of course I have."

"When? What was his name?"

"None of your business," I say, trying to keep the embarrassment out of my voice.

"Virgin."

"So what if I am?" I ask.

"Nothing," he says, grinning like it's the funniest thing he's ever heard. "I think the High Priestess magic must have picked the wrong person. It had to have made a mistake. Maybe that's why your spork won't obey you. You're a virgin. How are you supposed to control sexual energy when you have no experience with it?"

Shit. What if he's right? What if part of my problem is that I've never even done this as a normal person, not involving magic?

I'm not about to share my doubts, though. He's busy laughing his ass off, so I storm ahead and slip into Professor Darius's class, late again. When class ends, everyone files out, but I stay in my seat.

"Is everything all right, Jade?" Darius asks, hovering behind his desk.

Rocco sticks his head through the door. "Everyone out? Cool. I wanna be here for this."

He slips into the room and slides into an empty seat, an eager smile on his face while he waits.

I sigh, deciding to ignore him instead of giving him what he wants and rising to the bait.

"Someone must've broken into my room," I tell Darius. "Cleo is missing."

Darius clears his throat and glances between me and Rocco before coming around his desk. "That's not possible," he says, leaning against the front of his desk.

"Why not?"

"There's a spell on your room," he says. "No one can get in unless you invite them."

"Including your roommate," Rocco says.

I glare daggers at him, but Darius shows no surprise. Here we thought we were being so clever, but apparently everyone knows Elowen's living with me. Of course they do. How could I be such a dumbass?

"Besides the spell, one of us is always on guard," Rocco says. "Seriously, Jade. We know everything. You think you could keep something this big from us?"

"So all that shit about sharing was… What? A ploy to get me to open up to you about something you already knew?"

"Maybe I was hoping you'd ask me to share something about my life," Rocco says with a wink. And even though he says it in a joking way, I can't help but wonder if it's true. I don't know anything about him, really. All I know is that he's a royal pain in the ass, even if he's not quite the asshole he was when I started back in September.

Professor Darius clears his throat. "Regardless, there's no way someone could have broken in."

"So, the only person who could steal your spork is someone who already has access to your room," Rocco says, then coughs into his fist like he's trying to muffle the name he speaks. "Elowen."

"No fucking way," I say. "She's been nothing but sweet and kind to me since I got here. Unlike some people. And she's beyond grateful I let her share my room so she doesn't have to go dark. She'd never steal from me." I stand up as I speak, gathering my things with as much dignity as I can muster.

"How much you want to bet?" Rocco asks, a challenge in his eyes as he lounges in the desk, dwarfing its size with his bulky, muscular body.

I stare at him, then cross my arms. "Fine. If I'm right, you never give me shit again. Including calling me Cinderella, making fun of my magic, my weapon, my appearance, and anything else."

"Okay," Rocco says with a shrug. "And if I win, I get to take you on a date."

"A date?" I ask, balking for a second. Almost thinking he wants to spend time with me.

And then he grins and wets his lips. "That's right. A date. That includes everything I normally do on a first date."

I remember his crude comments about sex on a first date, and I stare back at him, not backing down from the challenge. "No way."

He shrugs and lazily peels himself up from the chair. "I thought you had total confidence in your friend."

"I do."

"If you really had no doubts, you'd bet."

I grit my teeth. "Fine. I accept."

"Jade..." Professor Darius says, his brow furrowing in concern.

"You're such hypocrites," I burst out. "You guys have dark magic, but you treat dark magic students like they're bad people. They're not. In fact, if anything, Elowen has been nicer to me than any one of the assholes you assigned to guard me."

"I asked if you were having trouble with them," Darius reminds me.

"Yeah, but you're prejudiced just like everyone else," I say. "If you weren't, you'd know that Elowen has ten times more good in her heart than all your strongest sorcerers. So yeah. Don't try to "protect" me after assigning those assholes to follow me around. Just because they're powerful doesn't mean they're good. Trust me on that one."

I pick up my books and march out the door, leaving him and Rocco behind. I hope he tears Rocco a new one when he finds out what a jerk they were to me for the first month I was here. On my way to my next class, I shoot Asher a text. As soon as I arrive, he pulls me to our table and hands me my wand.

"What happened?" he whispers as our teacher starts going on about the newest spell we're supposed to learn.

"My spork is missing," I say.

"Again?"

"Not again," I say, shooting him some stink eye. "Last time was different. This time… What if someone stole it?"

"Considering how stubborn it is, I don't think they'll get far with it," Asher says.

That makes me feel a little better. I mean, if Cleo wouldn't work with me for an entire month, and I'm the one she chose, I doubt she's going to cooperate with a stranger.

After a while, I turn to Asher. "Is there any way... I mean, you don't think Elowen would ever do something like that in a million years, right?"

Instead of answering with the adamant loyalty I expected, he twists his lips to the side and focuses on the sprout we're supposed to be making grow. After a minute, he says, "Honestly? I don't know, Jade. I want to say no, but maybe it's possible."

"Really?"

"Elowen's my best friend," he says slowly. "But she's been acting different ever since we got here. This necromancy stuff has really gotten to her. She thinks she's going dark. I mean, I love the girl, and I don't want to think she did it, but I wouldn't say it's absolutely impossible. Not anymore."

"Well, shit. I just bet my virginity on it."

"Girl. You didn't."

"I still don't think she'd do that to me. Not after I let her move in. She's been so much happier," I say, thinking of how

207

we stayed up late giggling over the ridiculousness of *My Fairytale Life* and arguing who was the hottest shifter in the world.

"Elowen has a good heart, but she can definitely be pushed around," Asher says. "I'm surprised she's held on this long without going totally dark. Her magic is part of her, just like ours. Can you honestly say your magic hasn't affected you since it was Unleashed?"

"Okay," I say slowly, my heart sinking. "I'll ask her, but I'm giving her the benefit of the doubt. She hasn't given me any reason to think she's untrustworthy."

The next few hours pass with painful slowness as I try to construct a conversation with Elowen that won't have her running away in tears and thinking I'm accusing her of being a thief.

By dinnertime, I have my speech memorized.

After we all sit down at our table in the cafeteria, I gather my nerve and go for broke. I turn to my friend and clear my throat. "Can I ask you something?"

She takes a bite of her spaghetti and wipes her mouth. "Yeah?"

"You haven't seen my spork around, have you?"

Elowen swallows in a gulp, her eyes widening. "No, why?"

"I can't find it."

"And you think I took it," she says, her shoulders slumping in defeat.

My heart tugs for her. She's so down on herself. "I didn't say that," I say gently. "I was just asking if you've seen it anywhere. I mean, we do share a room. If you saw it lying around somewhere..."

She sets her fork down with trembling fingers. "Don't you think if I had, I'd give it to you?"

"Elowen, I didn't say you had it," I say. "I only asked if you'd seen it."

"Everyone already thinks I'm evil. Even you. Admit it. You think I'd stab you in the back."

"I don't think you're evil," I say. "I know you have dark magic, but just like all of us, you can choose how to use that magic."

"But I can't choose," she says, a tear sliding down her cheek. "I'm dark. I can feel the darkness taking me over every day. You're right not to trust me. I'm not good." She jumps up and runs from the room.

"Elowen," I call, jumping to my feet.

Asher puts a hand on my arm to stop me. "You can't keep hiding her and taking care of her, Jade. She can't run away from her magic any more than you can."

"Seems to be the theme of the day," I mutter, casting one more longing glance at the door before returning to my seat. I push my food away, unable to eat after fighting with a friend.

"Maybe this is a good thing," Asher reasons. "She'll have to sort out her magic for herself, just like everyone else. I'll text and let her know we're here for her, but we can't do this for her."

"Tell her I'm sorry, and I don't think she took it," I say, nodding across the room at the table of mean girls. "My money's on one of the Bellas. I have swordplay class with Brunette Bella. Maybe she took it out of my bag."

"Asking her will probably go over even worse than asking Elowen."

We look across the room to the bitches I love to loathe, sitting with their bitchy friends on the other side of the cafeteria.

"Trust me, they're always first on my list of suspects."

Asher and I empty our trays and head back to our rooms for the evening.

Not five feet out of the cafeteria, Rocco's on my heels. "Why are you still eating with the necromancer?" he asks. "If you won't listen to me about who to hang out with, maybe you should take care of yourself and see how that goes."

"Fine by me," I say. "I didn't ask for your company."

He draws back, and the look on his face is… Hurt.

Fuck. I'm on a roll tonight.

We've gotten used to each other, and I thought our back-and-forth banter was fun for both of us, but for whatever reason, I've struck a nerve.

"Sorry," I mutter. Eating crow is not my style, but I'm a big girl, and I can apologize when I've hurt someone, even if he doesn't offer the same courtesy.

"No worries," he says. "I don't have feelings."

He drops back and follows from a distance as I walk with Asher back to the dorm, still mulling over my fight with Elowen.

"Do you think it's possible to get Elowen out of the House of Necromancy?" I ask.

"I don't know," Asher admits. "I mean, that's her magic. She has to learn to control it."

"I'll talk to Darius," I say. "There has to be something we can do. Surely necromancy can be used for good, and not just evil. Maybe we can convince them that Elowen can use her magic for light purposes."

"You're on a first name basis with Professor Hottie-Pants?" Asher asks with a grin.

"Shut up," I say, rolling my eyes.

"No, I think it's a great idea," he says. "Maybe you can bring it up next time you stay the night with him."

Chapter 16

I'm thankful that I have a friend like Asher who can make me laugh in the worst circumstances, but it doesn't last long. I hear Rocco take his place outside my room, working double duty after his classes to keep me safe. I offended him twice now, but I'm not sure how to deal with it. He's obviously more than the asshole I pegged him as.

And then there's Elowen. I should have handled that more delicately, knowing how sensitive she is. Direct might be my style, but it clearly isn't hers. As I lie in bed, I listen for her returning, but she doesn't come back. After getting used to her quiet snores, the room is too quiet without her. I send her a quick text apologizing, but I get nothing back but silence.

After a while, I get up and open the window, as if she's going to be hanging out on the fire escape waiting for an invite. Of course she's not.

With a sigh, I pull the window closed and sit on the edge of my bed staring at the door. Wanting to do something I'm sure I'll regret. But he's just outside the door. I can feel his presence there, as if he's just waiting for me to make the first move. I'm not sure I want to get involved with him any deeper than I am. I have enough on my plate with school, and Cleo, and knowing that when this is all over, I can't have a normal life. When everyone else goes off to start their lives after mastering their magic, I'll go back to Silas.

But of all the guys, Rocco is the one who won't care. It would mean something to Thorn, whether or not he'd admit it. He's been avoiding me since our night excursion, anyway. Ryker's too much of an asshole, and Darius… Well, that'll never happen.

But Rocco? He could definitely sleep in my bed without meaning or attachment. I can lay down the boundaries before we even start. I'm not planning on having sex, but if we get carried away because of my magic, well, he could handle that without attachment, too.

Taking a deep breath, I decide to go for it. I need some company tonight, and Rocco's the best one to do it. And just my luck, he's on guard duty. I crack open the door and peer out. Rocco is standing against the wall with a book open in one hand, a pencil stuck behind his ear. It's such a strange sight that I almost laugh. He looks up and quirks an eyebrow. "Planning another escape?"

"I'm lonely," I admit, giving him a hopeful look.

He gives a silent little snort. "I've got no advice for that one, Cinderella. I've never been lonely in my life."

"Liar."

He quirks an eyebrow again, closing his thick textbook this time. "What do you want, Jade?"

I take a breath and blurt out the truth. "I was hoping you'd come in."

A slow smile spreads over his gorgeous lips. "I thought you'd never ask," he says, swaggering across the hall and into my room. He drops his textbook—Advanced Sorcery—on the desk and kicks off his shoes before I've even shut the door.

Now that he's in my room, taking it over with his huge presence, I don't know what to do with myself. "So, how does this work?" I ask.

"Well, see, a man has this thing called a penis…" He stops at my desk to examine my dead orchid plant for a second, his eyes flicking to my family picture. I suddenly wish I hadn't invited him in.

"Not that," I say, rolling my eyes. "I'm not that naïve."

"Hey, you're still a virgin at eighteen," he says, holding up both hands and turning away from my desk. "For all I know you were raised by some crazy cult who had to sign off on it when it was cherry-popping time."

"Oh my god," I say, laughing through my embarrassment.

Rocco flops down on my bed and pats the space beside him. "Don't worry, I'll be gentle."

"Hey, you didn't win the bet yet," I say.

"Yet," he says with a Cheshire grin. "So, you admit I'm right. Your friend is the culprit."

"No," I say, taking a seat beside him. "How do I know you're not the one who stole it?"

216

"Why would I take your weapon?" he asks, his brows shooting up in surprise. It looks genuine.

"I don't know," I admit. It doesn't make sense. Why would the guys want my magic? They're around it enough already, and they certainly don't need any help finding girls.

"I don't need your sex magic, baby," Rocco says. "I got plenty of my own."

I shake my head to clear my thoughts. Being so close to him is doing funny things to me. "I'm just telling you that sex isn't on the table tonight, so you won't accuse me of being a tease when I stop you."

"You don't have a table, so I figured as much," he says, propping himself up on one elbow. "We can use the bed tonight. We'll save sex on the table for another night."

"I'm already regretting letting you step through my door."

"That's because I haven't gotten started," he says in a low rumble, running the back of his fingers down my arm. "Talking isn't where I excel."

Warm shivers race through my entire body at his touch. "And I thought I had the seductive magic," I say, closing my eyes.

"This isn't magic. It's one hundred percent me, baby." He lifts my hand and brings it to his lips. Our eyes meet, and when he presses a warm kiss to my skin, I sigh out loud. Maybe this is why I don't touch people. I seriously cannot handle it if a kiss on the hand can send me into a swoon.

"Then I think you better dial it back to like fifty percent," I breathe.

Rocco laughs and tugs at me to lie down. "I'll be good," he says, adjusting his position as I lift my feet and lie next to him on the bed.

"What if you can't?" I ask. "What if some of my magic escapes and..."

"And I can't control myself?" he asks, looking down at me from where he's still propped on his elbow.

"Well..."

"I want to say it's not a possibility," he says. "That I'd never hurt you. But... The truth is, with you, I don't know."

"Stupid magic," I mutter.

"I don't know if it's just the magic," he says. "You've been hard to resist since the second I laid eyes on you."

"You mean when I was elbow deep in a toilet, wearing my janitor clothes?"

"Never underestimate the power of janitor clothes," he says, a smile tugging at the corners of his lips as his fingers tickle my belly with gentle strokes.

"If I recall correctly, the only power they had was to make everyone treat me like shit," I say. "Including you."

"Ahh, I wasn't that bad, was I? I gotta rag on the new class a little. It's my right as a third-year student."

I roll my eyes. "Of course. You couldn't lose your reputation as a tough guy."

"Hey, I took so much shit as a freshman, you have no idea. Now it's my turn to dish it out. I earned it. One day you'll see all those baby-faced freshmen coming in, and you'll give them a hard time, too."

"That's a terrible excuse for treating people like shit."

"How about the fact that it freaked me out how much I wanted you," he says, leaning down to nuzzle my cheek. "And maybe I was a little butt hurt that you didn't seem to return the feeling."

"Even worse."

"Then I'm sorry," he says, scooting down beside me and sliding an arm around my waist. He wiggles his eyebrows and runs his tongue slowly along his lower lip. "How about you let me make it up to you?"

A shiver of pure lust shoots through me, swelling between my legs with a pressure that's now all too familiar. Damn it. If I get aroused, and my magic starts escaping…

Rocco leans down, his full lips brushing over mine. My hand slides around the back of his neck, pulling his mouth lower. I press my lips to his, relishing the softness of his mouth as it caressed mine. His mouth is confident and hungry on mine, moving quickly as he devours my kisses, tasting my lips and my tongue, running his tongue along the sharp edges of my teeth and swiping across the roof of my mouth. I moan against him, into him, my hands curling into fists in the back of his shirt.

"Take this off," I say, panting through the words as I tug at his shirt. He strips it off in two seconds flat, tossing it to the floor and resuming his position next to me. I run my fingers over his hot skin, the muscles under it dancing for my touch. God, even his muscles have muscles.

"You like that?" he asks, laughter in his voice. I'm too awed to give him shit about his ego. Because yeah, I like it. He looks like a freaking body builder. I've moved up in the world since the last time I made out with a guy—a scrawny freshman in high school who felt me up behind the field house. I'm more than happy to let Rocco know exactly how sexy he is, even if he already knows it.

After a minute, he rolls over onto me, rocking his hips gently against mine as he leans on his elbows and smiles down at me. "Say yes, Cinderella," he whispers. "Let me make you feel like a princess."

I nod, biting at my lower lip as our eyes meet. I've never done what he's suggesting, and I'm a little self-conscious at the thought. But when his lips graze mine again, and a shiver shoots straight to my core, I forget all about it. My clit throbs at the thought of those soft lips teasing it the way he's teasing my lips. He moves down, pressing my chin up and angling his mouth to my throat. His tongue swirls over my skin, his lips tugging as his tongue tastes. I run my fingers through his short, soft hair, my body alive with pleasure as his mouth moves lower, his scratchy chin nuzzling aside the neck of my T-shirt.

His lips close around my peaked nipple, and I gasp with pleasure. It feels as if a chord runs straight from my nipple to my clit, and when he gives a hard suck, I arch up, almost crying out. His mouth wets the fabric over my nipple, his tongue flicking at the sensitive nub.

I bite back a whimper as he slides down further. My core throbs for him, aching to be filled, and my legs part for his massive form as he moves lower, his hot mouth on my belly. He pushes up my T-shirt, his tongue flicking into my belly button, making me squirm for more as his thumbs skim across the tickling spot inside my hipbones. He grabs my hips, holding onto my curves as he descends even lower, mouthing my mound through the thin fabric of my panties. He doesn't have to wet those. They're already soaked, and he moans as he sucks at me through them, tasting my juices.

"Jade," he moans from between my thighs. "I'm going to lick your pussy until you scream my name."

Before I can begin to answer, he tugs my panties aside and thrusts his tongue into my wetness. I gasp, the sensation so deliciously sudden and shocking that I sit bolt upright.

Term 1: Unleashing Trials

Rocco's hand stops me, pushing me back as his mouth burrows against me, his hot tongue thrusting between my folds. Without stopping, he grabs my panties and tears them off, tossing the shredded cotton to the floor and driving his mouth deeper between my legs. He moans against me, his hands spreading my thighs, spreading my lips, his tongue going straight for the center of me.

My head drops back, and a little cry escapes my lips as he forces his tongue past my opening.

Oh. God.

No one has ever touched me here before, and the sensation is like nothing I've ever experienced. I can't hold back the cries as his tongue plunges into me again and again. His fingers slide through my wetness, pinching my clit while his tongue fucks me, and heat explodes through my body. His name tears from my lips, and waves of shimmering light rip through my whole body, gripping me in the helpless clutch of climax.

I'm still in a daze, pulses flicking through my center, when Rocco jumps off the bed like there's a snake in it.

He looks at me for one second, his eyes glazed and crazy, and then turns and blasts out the door so fast it bangs back open.

"Rocco," I call, sitting up and grabbing for the nearest thing to cover me. I come up with his shirt, which he didn't bother to pick up on his way out. I scramble from the bed and close and lock the door, still too stunned by the orgasm that is barely finished to think clearly. I drop back onto the bed, too confused to make sense of any of it. I press Rocco's shirt to my nose, but another smell invades my nostrils, so I burrow deeper into the smell of his shirt—deodorant and a hint of laundry detergent and something deeper, masculine, spicy. Something all Rocco.

The sweet smell is so insistent I can't block it out, though. I sit up and see the plant on my desk has been transformed. Instead of a wilted brown thing beyond all hope, I have a huge orchid so big it nearly overflows the pot, with a bloom stalk bursting with vibrant red blossoms, their ruffled edges glowing like sunshine.

What is happening to me?

I dive into bed, curl into a ball, and bury my face in Rocco's shirt. I don't want to think about any of it. It's all too much. I have no clue what just happened, but I can't forget the look on Rocco's face before he bolted, the eyes of a madman staring back at me. I just wanted a distraction, but Rocco is so much more than that. The worst part is, now that I've figured that out, it's too late. I have a sinking feeling that I just fucked up any chance of things going back to normal.

Chapter 17

The next morning, my door bursts open and Ryker strides in and yanks off my blanket, per usual. I don't know why I even bother locking. The locks in this place are clearly no match for the sorcerer's magic.

I sit up and rake my fingers through my blonde tangles as I try to wake up. "Where's Rocco?"

"He's——." Ryker breaks off and swallows, his eyes narrowing. "Where's your spork?"

"Still missing," I say with a sigh, throwing the blankets off my legs.

"Fuck," Ryker says, rubbing his temples. "Pretty soon I'll have to trail around after you with a hard-on all day like a teenager with raging hormones."

"Sorry for the inconvenience," I say, stomping over to my dresser and grabbing some clothes. "I'm not the one who asked for a guard."

"It's necessary now more than ever," he says.

"Why now?" I ask.

Ryker eyes my legs, which are long and bare, and I suddenly remember I'm not wearing anything under my T-shirt. A jolt of heat darts between my legs, and my nipples harden at the thought.

Ugh, okay, that's why. Because I'm horny as fuck, even after last night. Because I want him as much as I want the others.

"Your magic isn't finite," Ryker says. "You channel a kind of magic that exists in the world already. If you can't transfer it to your weapon…"

"How can I stop channeling it?" I ask.

"You can learn to," he growls.

I glare back at him and shove the drawer closed with my hip. "I'm trying."

"Are you? Or are you trying to drive us all insane?"

"Fuck you."

"Gladly." He takes one long stride forward and slides a hand behind my head, his body melding with mine in all the right places. I stare up at him, too shocked and breathless to protest. I can feel his cock stiffening against me, can feel the muscles of his body coiled with tension as they strain against me through my thin T-shirt. My fingers curl around his arms involuntarily. His biceps are taut, the muscles tight and trembling under my palms.

"I would ruin you for other men," he murmurs. "And I'd be glad." His gaze smolders into mine, his eyes so intense it makes my thighs tremble. "Is that what you want?"

"No," I whisper.

"That's what I thought," he says, stepping back and snatching up the clothes I dropped. He shoves them roughly into my hands, turns on his heel, and walks out, slamming the door behind him.

I turn toward the mirror, my legs trembling. What is happening? Where is Cleo when I need her? I obviously have too much magic right now, even after last night. This can't just be me. I tear through the drawers, emptying every last one, ransacking my desk, flipping my mattresses, hoping against desperate hope that she was here all along. But there is no Cleo. Finally, I sink down in the middle of the disaster and cry.

Then, I get up and get ready for classes, because Ryker is waiting outside my door and if I can't give Cleo my magic, maybe there's another way to get rid of it. For the first time in my life, I wish I didn't have magic. My magic isn't a gift. It's a curse.

*

"You gotta help me," I say to Darius that afternoon. I've arrived at our afternoon session empty handed, still missing Cleo.

"Jade," he says, a smile spreading across his lips that makes my heart flutter.

"Hi," I breathe. I have got to stop crushing on all these men.

"What can I help you with?" he asks, leaning back in his chair and linking his hands behind his head.

"Is there any way you can find Cleo?" I ask. I didn't realize I had become so attached to my weapon, but now that she's gone, her absence is like a constant itch. Like a phantom limb that is no longer there, but who I constantly miss.

Darius frowns. "I can try," he says, leaning forward and clasping his hands on his desk. "I suspect that if it was really stolen, someone has put some strong protection on it."

"Aren't you stronger than anyone here?" I ask.

He smiles a bit. "It doesn't work exactly like that. If a spell is laid first, it's very hard to break, even for a stronger magician."

"Last time, Thorn had it," I say. "Do you think…?"

Darius's frown deepens. "They got quite a lecture about that," he says. "I don't think they'd make that mistake again."

I slump into a seat, defeated. Not that I thought any of them had it. It's one thing for them to take it after I threw it away, thinking they'd teach me a lesson. That was a dick move, sure, but it's another thing for them to break into my room when I'm not there and steal from me. They may be assholes, but I don't think they're thieves. That takes a level of sneakiness that I don't see them sinking to.

"Is there any other way?" I ask. "Ryker said I could learn to, I don't know, harvest it from the world around me, or spend it somehow."

Darius clears his throat and starts straightening his desk. "Yes, well," he says, clearing his throat again. "Like anyone else's, your magic needs time to replenish when you use it."

"What does that mean?"

He loosens his tie and leans back, tenting his hands in front of his chest. "Remember when your magic was unleashed?"

"Vividly."

"And how... Intense it was. For you and those around you, who were within the radius of its reach. And then afterwards, you were able to function for quite a while without being... Overwhelmed by it again."

"True," I say. "I didn't try to hump anyone for at least a month."

Darius chuckles. "By the time it had recharged within you, you could transfer it to your vessel for safekeeping. That's how it works for all students. The Unleashing can be chaotic and a bit dangerous, but that burst of magic ensures it won't build back up until they have learned to control its flow a little better. And every time you use magic, like any other energy, it takes time to recharge. You couldn't run a marathon every day. You need time to recover. So, if you want to lessen the magic that is building within you, you'll need to expend some of it."

"My wand skills are a bit lacking, but I can light a candle with it," I say.

Darius loosens his tie a bit further and clears his throat. "I think you know that's not how your type of energy is spent."

My face warms as his gaze stays fixed on me. Yep, I know how to use sexual energy. I know because every time I've gotten worked up, it's fucked with everyone around me, just like at the Unleashing. When I use it, I might be able to release some of it, but then everyone around me is affected.

"That doesn't seem fair," I say. "I can't just, like, magically seduce someone. Because that's what it would be like. Getting them all intoxicated by my magical energy and taking advantage of them? Yeah, not really on board with that."

Professor Darius shifts around and leans forward, resting his elbows on his desk. "That's possible, I suppose," he says. "Or you could choose someone with whom you share a mutual attraction when you're not bewitching them with your magic."

Our eyes lock, and I'm sure he's talking about himself. About us.

This time, it's my turn to gulp. "What if…" I begin, my voice barely above a whisper. "What if you could teach me how to release it safely?"

"Jade…" A hundred emotions seem to be flickering in his eyes. Among them is a strong current of desire. He wants me. I can see it clear as day, clear as I want him.

"I like you," I blurt out. "A lot. I want this. And I think you want it, too."

"You're a student," he murmurs, his gaze smoldering with restrained longing. But he doesn't deny it.

"And you're a good teacher," I say, my courage bolstered. "And I've never… I mean, I could use some teaching."

"You're eighteen."

"And you can't be much over thirty," I say. "Old enough to know what you're doing, but not too old for me. I don't care about age."

We stare at each other as we speak, not breaking eye contact.

"I could lose my job."

"I don't want that," I concede, slumping back in my chair. "I didn't realize."

"I'm flattered, Jade. I won't deny the temptation is there."

"How do I know if the attraction is because of magic or not?" I ask, segueing to a safer topic.

"You know because you're still interested even when you aren't using your magic," Darius says. "You're an attractive woman, Jade. I'm sure you have no trouble attracting men without using your magic."

"So being around my magic, it's like a contact high," I say. "It comes out whenever I work with it intentionally or when I get… Excited."

"It seems so," Darius says, color rising to this throat. "When you're sexually stimulated, such as the incident at the club."

Great. Every time I orgasm, I'm going to make dudes go insane.

"And if I'm using magic every day in your class, you get a dose of it each time? And so does Ryker, when I work with Cleo."

"Yes," he says. "As does everyone in class. There seems to be an unusual amount of students coupling up this year."

He's smiling, but I can't help but blush. I mean, I'm making everyone in my classes horny. At least they're not all lusting after me, but still. It's a little weird.

"So, what you're telling me is to find a boyfriend?"

He swallows, his Adam's apple bobbing. "Or your sword."

Huh. That's the first time someone has called Cleo a sword instead of a spork. Maybe it's time I start seeing her differently, too. I already know she means more to me than I ever knew, that I miss her terribly. But needing her and respecting her are two separate things, and it might be time to start treating her with a little more appreciation. I vow to do that the moment I get her back. If only I knew where she was and how to get her back.

In the meantime, apparently I need to get laid.

Chapter 18

"Don't look now," Asher says the next day at dinner as we slide into our seats.

"At what?" I twist around in my seat, and my heart stops.

"You looked," Asher says with a sigh.

Unlike lunch times, dinner is a come-and-go as you want affair. And right now, here comes a couple I never wanted to see. Blonde Bella hangs on Rocco's massive, muscular arm, smiling up at him like he's a rock star. But that's not what makes me sick. What makes me sick is that Rocco is smiling back at her.

And not in that indulgent, "let this skank finish making her case so I can escape" way that Thorn does.

"I'm sure it's just a fling," Asher says. "She never keeps her men for long. Trust me on that. There's been a lot of them. They always see through her hotness to the ugly person she is within."

"She doesn't like Rocco," I say. "She's using him."

Asher takes a drink of water. "Sorry, Jade."

I turn to my most reserved guard, who sits at the next table. "Come sit with us," I say, patting the table beside me.

"This should be interesting," Asher says, glancing from Thorn to Bella, who is always watching him.

Thorn looks up from his food, a startled look on his face. "Now?"

"I won't bite," I say. "You spend half your day trailing around after me. Don't you think it would be less boring if you talked to me?"

He pauses for a second, a calculating look on his face.

I sigh. "I want to ask you about Rocco, okay? I'm not going to put my magic juju on you."

Bella belts out a laugh that's so high-pitched that even from across the room, I can tell it's false. I glance up to find her staring at us even as she clings to Rocco at their table. She's halfway in his lap while he scarfs down his salad.

Seemingly oblivious to her jealousy, Thorn scoots back his chair and moves his plate and cup over to our table with no comment and no visible reaction to my words. Okay, then. He's a tough nut to crack, but that doesn't mean I can't ask him what I want to know.

Before I can ask, he speaks. "I'm sorry about what happened at that party."

"What? The kick-off party?" I ask, surprised since that was ages ago. We've barely said two words to each other since, but still. It's all but forgotten to me.

"Yes," he says, frowning down at his salad.

"You're sorry about… Dancing with me?" I ask, trying not to let that hurt.

"I should have been watching out for you," he says. "It's my job."

"Not that night," I remind him. "I wasn't even supposed to be there. You were out at a party, having fun. You were off duty. Rocco was the one on guard duty."

"You could have been hurt." Thorn forks through his salad with a fierce frown.

I start to answer, but Asher elbows me and nods toward the table across the room where Bella is straddling Rocco's lap.

Jealousy rears its ugly head inside me, but so does confusion and hurt. It's been two days since I've seen Rocco. He hasn't been on guard duty. The last time I saw him, we were sharing a moment more intimate than I've ever shared with anyone. And then he bolted so fast he didn't even get his book or his clothes, and now he's rubbing my enemy in my face.

I turn back to Thorn. "I'm the one who asked you to dance," I remind him. "So if that's what you're being weird about, you can stop now."

He nods and takes a bite of salad, still not looking at me. I realize then that the reason he doesn't talk to me isn't because he doesn't like me. And he's not a snob. If he were, he'd probably like Bella. No, he doesn't like me because I make him uncomfortable. Maybe even scare him. My magic does, anyway. It's one thing he can't control, no matter how powerful he is.

"I'm sorry I let my magic get away from me that night," I say, reaching for his hand before thinking better of it and

239

drawing back. "And I'm really sorry that I dragged you back to my dad's and got you hurt that night."

He shrugs. "I'm fine."

"I shouldn't have gone at all," I say. "It was stupid. It probably put more attention on Dad, and that's the last thing I wanted. I just wanted to see him."

"I get it," he says. "He's your dad."

Asher kicks me under the table, and I turn to him. While Thorn's head is lowered over his food, Asher gives a quick nod in his direction and puts two fingers to his temple like a gun. "His dad," he mouths.

Fuck. Something inside me twists painfully. So that's why he took me. That's why he was concerned about me when we first got here, and I was freaking out about my dad.

"Well, I'm sorry I dragged you into it," I say. "And thank you for taking me."

This time, I don't pull back. I lay my hand on top of Thorn's. He stares at it for a second, and my heart skips as I wait for him to pull away. After a moment, he turns his hand, lacing his fingers through mine, and squeezes. My heart thuds in my chest. How can I have this connection with him, but also feel like my insides are spaghetti being twisted around a fork when I look over and see Rocco's hands spread over Bella's ass as she kneels over his lap?

"You were going to say something about that dumbass?" Thorn asks, his gaze following mine.

"You know she's using him to get to you," I say.

Thorn almost chokes, then covers his mouth with a fist and changes it to a cough. "What?"

"Dude, Bella has been in love with you for like a decade," Asher says, rolling his eyes.

"And she thinks I'm going to like her if she fucks my friend?"

"She's trying to make you jealous," I say.

"That only works if the person likes you," he says, eyeing me.

"But she's using him," I say. "Surely he knows that."

"Like I said," Thorn murmurs, pulling his hand from mine. "Making someone jealous only works if they like you."

"What does that mean?" I ask. "You think Rocco is with Bella now to make me jealous?"

Thorn shrugs. "If not, he looks pretty happy to be used."

It's true. Now they're making out. It's all I can do not to throw something and tell them to get a room. Of course Bella's rubbing it in my face, but does Rocco have to? This isn't to make me jealous. This is beyond that. This is meant to hurt me.

And it works. It fucking hurts. But what did I expect when I invited him in? Did I honestly think he cared about me? He's always been an asshole. Why stop at teasing? Why not make me think he liked me, only to dump me for my enemy? Why not get me to trust him with my body the way I've never trusted anyone, only to completely stop speaking to me? It's the oldest story in the book.

I know a thing or two about being used now, too, thanks to him. Why should I care if someone else is using him? And if he really is doing it to hurt me, then Bella's the one being used.

"You know what?" I say to Thorn. "You're right. He deserves it."

"Or maybe he can't have the one he wants," Asher says, cutting his eyes at me. "So he's making do."

"Right," I say. "Because that looks like a guy who's pining over another woman." I nod to where he and Bella are leaving, laughing and nearly skipping as they hurry out, probably because they can't wait to hook up.

"You could probably join them if you want," Thorn says. "Rocco's always good for a good time."

"Ha, yeah," I say. "I'll pass."

"The guy likes to have fun," Thorn says, stabbing at his chicken like it offended him. "If that's what you're looking for, you won't have to wait long. My friend has a notoriously short attention span when it comes to women."

"What if that's not what I'm looking for?" I ask.

"Then you probably won't get it from him," he says. "But you still won't have to wait long to find out."

"Ouch," Asher says. "Can you say *truth hurts*?"

"Would you stop?" I ask. "You act like I'm in love with Rocco or something."

Asher arches one pierced eyebrow at me.

"I'm not," I protest, but I can feel my face warming. I have utterly no idea why.

On the way back to the dorms, Asher squeezes my arm and leans in, lowering his voice. "I didn't want to press it in front of

Thorn, since it seems like he has the hots for you, but you totally are in love with Rocco."

"Am not," I protest.

"I think you're in love with all of them."

My mouth drops open with indignation. "You think I'm a slut like Bella."

"No, but I think you're in serious need of a good dicking."

"Why does everyone keep saying that?"

Asher laughs. "Deny it all you want, but every time their names come up, it's written all over your face. If that's a secret you want to keep, you need to work on your poker face."

Find Cleo, get laid, develop poker face... My to-do list is getting longer by the day. Maybe it's time I check something off the list.

Chapter 19

The next few weeks are not my finest. Elowen avoids both me and Asher, keeping to her House of Necromancy friends. At least I hope she's made friends. I don't see a lot of her. Unfortunately, I see all too much of Bella. She flounces around giving me smug smiles and fawning over Rocco. He's sickeningly smitten with her, and though he returns to guard duty, he trails behind me like Thorn.

I have to admit, I miss him. I miss our flirting. Thorn always walks silently behind, and Ryker strides ahead like he can't be bothered with me, like he's always pissed. But Rocco always walked with me, like he was a friend instead of a guard, there only because he was employed to be. Even when he was an asshole, and he tried to cut me down, it felt like we were equals.

After all, I can dish out as well as I can take it. After a while, it kinda became our thing. Now that I don't have it, I realize how much I enjoyed our little game of taking shots at each other.

I try to talk to him a couple times, but he just laughs it off, saying Bella won't like it. Besides that change, there's the lack of Cleo to contend with. I can still use my wand in spells class, and learn about magic with Professor Darius, but Ryker's class is a nightmare. It's not easy going to swordplay every day without a sword. At last, he agrees to lend me a regular, non-magical sword. It's a challenge, but I steadily improve under his relentless, brutal training.

I don't have my private lessons with the professor, which makes things a little easier on both of us in the self-control department. He pulls me aside one day and tells me that as he suspected, someone has a spell on Cleo. The best I can do is continue training and mastering my own magic without the help of a vessel to contain it and supply more when needed.

Controlling my magic may not be the easiest task, but observing other's reactions to my presence has taught me a lot. Especially as magic builds within me. Since it's now impossible to store some of my energy away, it grows every day, showing like a neon sign. Pretty soon, random guys start trailing around after me, and I'm completely relieved and grateful to have guards who can apparently control themselves.

And a best friend who has no interest in pussy, magical or not.

"The Winter Ball is coming up," Asher says to me one night as we're watching a movie on his laptop. "Think you can convince Professor Hottypants to let you go?"

"Doubtful," I say. "I'm pretty much walking around like a cat in heat. I want to hump everyone, and apparently the feeling is mutual."

Asher laughs. "Glad I can be the exception."

"Yeah, how come my magic doesn't affect you?" I ask. "That's not fair."

"Oh, girl," he says. "Trust me, I've been affected."

I draw back and grab the popcorn away from him. "Spill, or you get no popcorn."

"Just because I don't want *you* doesn't mean I'm not horny as hell," he says. "Whoops, did that come out mean?"

It's my turn to laugh. "Actually, right now I really appreciate someone not wanting me. I'm pretty sure Black-Haired Bella made a pass at me today."

"Okay, first off, gross," Asher says. "And secondly, just because you're too uptight to get laid doesn't mean anyone else is. I'm getting plenty, don't you worry."

"What? Who?"

"No one special," he says, snagging the bowl back. "I promise to let you know if I start seeing someone."

"How are you having more sex than me?"

"Jade, honey," he says. "Everyone on this campus is having more sex than you."

"Really?"

"I live in a boy's dorm," he says, giving me an 'oh please' look. "And in case you hadn't noticed, I'm a total hottie. Of course I'm getting laid. You should really try it. Don't take this the wrong way, but I think you need to release some of that magic. Everyone's starting to chafe."

"Oh my god." I cover my face and flop back on the pillows. "I'm going to have to find someone to have sex with me. How do you even do that?"

Asher stares at me. "Um, you walk outside, girlie."

"I don't want some random guy who's attracted to my magic."

"Why not?"

"It's weird. It's like I've drugged them."

"Then pick someone you liked before. You're the one who always says you can choose what to do with your magic. So choose someone. You're a knockout, Jade. It's not like you wouldn't have options even without your magic. In fact, there's a guy outside your door who would probably blow your mind if you'd let him."

When I think of Ryker standing out there, more than my heart thumps. A throb goes straight to my clit. Ryker blowing my mind might be earth shattering. Or it might destroy me.

"Do you even know who my guard is tonight?" I ask Asher.

He looks me up and down and raises his eyebrows. "No. And that's exactly my point."

"Stop that," I say, grabbing the popcorn back. "Let's just watch the movie."

But I can't stop thinking about the man outside my room. The man I want so badly, and who said he wanted me, too.

From the way he's treated me, though, I have a feeling I want something entirely different from what he wants. And if I offered him what he wants, he'd turn me down just for the joy of hurting me one more time.

*

The next morning, as he walks me to class, Ryker strides ahead as always.

"Hey, can I ask you something?" I say, jogging to catch up.

"What?" he snaps.

"I was thinking," I begin. "You know how Silas sent that demonling after me? What if he wasn't trying to kill me? What if he was after Cleo the whole time?"

"Silas doesn't have Cleo."

"How do you know?" I ask, giving him some serious side eye.

He's silent a minute, his strong jaw clenched. He stares straight ahead as we cross campus. "I paid him a visit already."

"You did?" I ask, drawing up in surprise. Ryker doesn't break his stride, so I have to run to join him again. "When?"

"After she went missing," he says. "The guy was pissing himself by the time we left. He couldn't have lied if he wanted."

"Oh." I'm not sure what to say to that. Did Ryker actually do something nice for me?

"Don't look so shocked," he says, though he hasn't even glanced my way, so he can't possibly know my expression. "There's no one on this campus who wants you to find your sword more than I do."

I gulp at the meanings his words could carry. I shouldn't ask, but I can't help myself.

"Because I need it for your class?" I peek at him from the corner of my eye, my heart thudding as I wait for his answer.

"Because you're a distraction," he snaps.

Okay then. Not that I expected him to say anything different, but... Maybe I hoped. I don't know what's wrong with me. I can't seem to get him off my mind, but I have some other connection with Thorn, and then I'm jealous as hell and hurt about Rocco, so obviously I like him, too. Again, I blame the magic. That has to be it.

"You don't seem very distracted," I say after taking a moment to recover my ego. "You're the most focused person in this place."

"I *was* focused," Ryker says, halting so fast I'm several steps ahead before I register that he's stopped. "Until you."

I wheel around, my temple pounding with anger. I'm so sick of being blamed for this shit. "Excuse me?"

"I want to fuck you," he says, stepping forward, invading my space with his presence and heat, his imposing height, his angular jaw and piercing eyes. Everything about him makes me tremble, and my anger dissolves. I'm not sure if the feeling that replaces it is excitement or fear or both. Ryker grabs my chin and pulls it up, squeezing so hard my lips pucker up and my eyes are forced to meet his. "I want to fuck you every second of every day for the rest of my life."

"You do?" I whisper.

"And it still wouldn't be enough," he says, enunciating each word. "So forgive me if I'm a little resentful of the intrusion of your magic into my life."

With that, he turns and storms off, leaving me to trail behind like usual. But today, my mind is reeling. Ryker hates that I'm here. He hates that I distract him. I knew he wasn't my biggest fan, but it still hurts to have it spelled out so plainly. He doesn't like me. He doesn't want me here.

I enter the training studio only to see that in the thirty seconds it took me to make it there, Black-Haired Bella has already attached herself to his arm. I try to ignore them as I go to put my bag in the cubbies and get my dummy sword, but they're standing right there, as if Bella accosted him the moment he walked in.

"I thought we went over this," Ryker says to her. "You're too young for me."

"I'm legal," she purrs. "Barely."

Hurl.

"I don't have time for this," Ryker says.

"But it'll be the three power couples on campus," she says. "We're the last one in the trifecta."

I almost snort out loud. Does she honestly think Ryker gives a fuck about how people see him?

"I'm not interested in being a power couple," he says.

Called it, I think, smiling to myself.

"You're not the only one on this campus who's suffering," she says. "I feel it, too, Ryker. I need it, too."

I glance over, and she catches the movement and quickly looks back at my sorcerer. She strokes his bicep, fluttering her lashes at him. "I'll let you fuck me anywhere, any way you want."

I just about choke on my spit at her words. What the actual fuck. Is this how the other Bella got Rocco? Because he was definitely needing something when he left my room that night. If he ran into her, and she offered… I mean, Asher pretty much told me as much, but hearing a girl say it like that, so bluntly, throws me for a loop. If that's what the guys at the academy want, I'm never going to get laid. There's no way in hell I can compete with that.

I realize Ryker hasn't answered, and I look up to find his eyes on me. A throb of longing goes through me. I straighten from cramming my stuff in the cubby and grab my sword.

Say no, I want to shout. *Say you want me instead.*

Bella sees where he's looking, though. For one second, her gaze meets mine, and she narrows her eyes with pure hatred. Then she turns her attention back to Ryker, tugging at his arm.

"If that's who you want, you can put a bag over my head and call me her name."

My shock must register on my face, but I don't know if Ryker sees it before he turns away.

"Fine," he says. "I'll see you tonight."

With that, he turns and strides to the center of the room to give instruction to the students beginning to trickle in. Bella flicks her hair back and smirks at me.

"And that," she says smugly. "Is how it's done."

Suddenly, the entire semester of rage boils up inside me. The way they called me a whore because of my magic, when she's going around offering to let a guy fuck her in the ass with a bag over her head. The frustration in knowing I'm not that brazen, and the hurt in seeing that it works. The pain of rejection from both him and Rocco. And worst of all, the fact that Bella's using my second-hand magic to get him. Because he has needs, and he can't have me. Because she's letting him pretend she's me when he fucks her.

The raging storm of emotion inside me is too much. It overwhelms me. Before I know what I'm doing, I fly at Bella. She shrieks when I slam into her, knocking her to the rubber flooring we practice on. I jump on her, slapping her hard across the face. She grabs my hair and wrenches it as hard as she can. Pain bolts through me, but I hardly feel it. I try to yank away, the momentum rolling us onto our sides. I punch her, and she punches back. She rolls me over onto my back, slapping me on both cheeks before I get in another blow.

We roll around for a good five minutes before I slap the shit out of Bella hard enough that someone grabs me and drags me off.

"As hot as that was, I think that's enough," Ryker says in my ear as he bodily carries me off the floor. "I can't have someone getting seriously injured in my class."

"Hot?" I ask, jerking away from him as he deposits me in an office off the side of the practice floor. "You think it's hot to see me beat the shit out of your date?"

"I'd prefer if you were both naked and covered in oil," he says with a smirk, tossing me a towel. "But yeah, two girls fighting is pretty hot."

"You're a pig."

He shrugs. "I'm a guy who has to spend eight hours a day in your circle of sex magic. You're lucky I haven't lost my damn mind."

"Obviously you have if you're seeing her," I shoot back.

"What would you have me do, Jade? Are you going to satisfy the needs your magic puts in all of us?"

I gulp, remembering Rocco and Thorn sandwiching me on the dance floor the night I had my first orgasm. How I fantasized we were all wearing a lot less in that moment.

"There's three of you," I mutter.

"You think you couldn't take us all? You're a fucking priestess, Jade."

"What does that mean?"

"It means you could have anyone on this campus who you wanted. So don't pull that shit with me. If you're not willing to fill our needs, you can't blame us for having to get it elsewhere after you drive us over the edge."

"So, it's my fault you're fucking my enemy?"

"Are you offering to do the job?"

I stand there staring at him. Finally, I shake my head. Not like that I'm not. Not when it's like some kind of transaction.

"That's what I thought," Ryker says, heading for the door.

"Have fun fucking that snake," I call after him. "I hope you don't get any diseases."

When he's gone, I wipe my face off with the towel and toss it in a laundry hamper in the corner for workout towels. I look out at the class, all of them focusing and working hard, and I know I can't go out there and spread my pheromones around and distract everyone. If I can't put my magic in Cleo, it's time I find some other solution.

At the end of the day, I head to Professor Darius's classroom and find him just locking the door. He has a leather messenger bag slung over one shoulder and is looking so good I could cry.

"Hello, Jade," he says, offering me a warm smile. "What can I do for you today?"

"You can let me go to the Winter Ball," I say, falling into step beside him as he heads out. It strikes me that I have no idea where he lives. I assume the guys live in the dorms, since they're students, but I have no idea if the teachers even live on campus.

Darius clears his throat. "I don't know if that would be wise right now."

"Then help me release some of this magic." My heart drums in my ears while I wait for him to cut me off. "And don't say I'm a student, and you're a teacher. I'm well aware, and I don't care."

"I'm twelve years older than you," he says.

I shrug. It matters less than nothing to me. I'm glad. I'm glad to have someone who won't make fun of me afterwards or run off with my enemy to spite me. "I may only be eighteen, but I've experienced a lot," I remind him. "You said so yourself. I just haven't experienced this."

"Which is the only kind of experience I shouldn't give you."

"Actually, as my teacher, you're supposed to help me contain my magic. If I don't have Cleo, isn't it your responsibility to teach me alternative methods?" I ask. "Think of it as magical training, nothing more."

Professor Darius sighs and runs a hand through his bronze colored hair. "I don't know if I could do that, Jade," he murmurs.

My heart leaps into my throat. I feel so pathetic for it, but after watching two of my sorcerers run off with the Bellas, hearing that someone might actually like me means way too much to me.

"Could you try?" I ask in a small voice.

He's quiet a long minute. Finally, he nods. "I know how much you want to go to the ball like the other students."

"I really do," I say. But it's so much more than that. I want him. I want him to be the one.

We walk in silence for a minute before he speaks. "We'll need some boundaries," he says. "Starting with, no sex."

"What?" I ask, balking. "I thought that's how…"

"You can release your magic without intercourse," he says. "As you've done before."

Before I know it, we've arrived back at my dorm, where Darius tells me to come by after my last class on Friday so he can help release my magic before the party.

I muse on that for the next few days. If I have an orgasm, it releases magic, which makes my magic weaker afterward. Which means the morning after Rocco gave me oral, I was at an all-time low. That was the morning Ryker said he wanted me. It wasn't because my magic was ridiculously high. It wasn't my magic at all. Ryker wants *me*. But how can I trust him if he'd go fuck someone else instead of waiting for me?

I can't. And if I can't trust him not to run off with Bella, then I can't trust him with my body. Right now, the only one I trust is Professor Darius. Every time I think of what he offered my heart speeds and my core clenches with excitement.

Finally, the evening before the ball, I work up my nerve and head to see him. I tap on the open door of his classroom, and he looks up and smiles.

"I need some help," I say, feeling suddenly flushed. "The Winter Ball is tomorrow."

"Ah," Professor Darius says, nodding. His gaze settles on my guard for the day. "You're dismissed. Enjoy your evening."

Thorn frowns, glancing between me and Darius. "I have another six hours of duty."

"I'll make sure Jade is safe," Darius says. "Take the night off."

Thorn turns to me, still looking troubled. "Call me if you need… Anything."

"I will," I say, a lump in my throat for some reason.

After one more long look, Thorn turns and slips off down the hall.

"Come in," Darius says.

I take a deep breath, step through the door, and close it behind me.

Chapter 20

For a minute, Professor Darius and I stand staring at each other as if measuring the other for a fight.

"I think you know why I'm here," I say at last, my voice coming out less sure than I intended.

Darius clears his throat. "I think I do," he says, stepping around the end of his desk.

"Can you show me how?" I ask. "I need to get rid of some of this magic, and…"

"You don't know how to pleasure yourself?" he asks.

The words send a spiral of lust through me. I'd rather him pleasure me, but I can't say it. I just shake my head, feeling the heat rise to my cheeks.

Professor Darius pauses, eyeing the door behind me.

"Show me?" I ask, stepping forward, closing the distance between us.

"I want to make an excuse," Darius says, gazing down at me. "I should say no."

"But you're not?" I ask, toying with the buttons on his dress shirt as I peek up at him from under my lashes.

He swallows, his dark eyes smoldering down at me. "The truth is, I don't think I can resist you one more day," he admits, his hands falling to my hips. "But are you sure this is what you want?"

"I've barely thought of anything else since you offered," I whisper.

Darius reaches behind me and locks the door, hitting the light next to it. The room is plunged into dimness, with only the afternoon light coming in around the edges of the curtains.

"I think about you every moment of every day, Jade," he says, tucking a strand of my hair behind my ear. "But we can't be together in the way you think."

"Because of your job?"

"I would give up more than that," he says. "I would give up my life to be inside you and feel you cum with my name on your lips."

A lightning bolt of heat strikes my blood at his words, sending a current of electricity through my body. My thighs clench as slickness coats my sex, and I grip his arms to keep my knees from giving way.

"I want you," I whisper, my words so inadequate after what he said, but he's done what he said with other women, has experience. I'm a naïve virgin.

"The one thing I can't risk is hurting you," he murmurs. "And I can't trust myself not to lose control and do that. Not with you."

"Then what?" I ask.

"My job is to teach you," he says. "I'll show you the easiest way to release your magic on your own, so you won't need me every time. I can't in good conscience do more than that."

I nod, feeling the tension coiled in his muscles, like a spring that might unleash and wash me away, drown me in his desire. Suddenly, I understand the guys having to be with other girls. I'm glad they are. I'm glad they have something to release this unbearable ache inside that feels like I'm going to die if I can't satisfy it. I only wish I could release Professor Darius's the way he's helping me.

"So, how do we start?" I ask, eyeing his neat charcoal slacks and blue button-up. All I want to do is tear them off, to see him and touch him and…

He clears his throat and gestures to his desk. "Why don't we start with a little visualization," he says.

So not how I imagined this going. But I do as he says because he's the instructor here.

I hop up on the edge of his desk and clasp my hands around my knee. "Okay. What should I visualize?"

Professor Darius stops in front of me and smiles slightly as he looks down at me. "What turns you on, Jade?"

"What?" I ask, hating how stupid and young I sound. I want to be brazen like the Bellas, to be experienced in the way he wants, so he wouldn't tell me he couldn't be with me. But I'm not. I'm not any of those things. All I feel right now is vulnerable.

"Do you trust me?" Darius murmurs, his eyes searching mine.

"Yes," I answer without hesitation. He's the one person here besides Asher who I fully trust, who has never done anything to make me suspect he'd do anything but protect me. He'd protect me even if it means giving up his own happiness—and mine.

"Close your eyes," he says.

I obey.

His hands land on my bare knees, setting fire to my skin. I gasp. Darius spreads my knees with one swift, firm movement. He steps between my knees, and I lean back on my palms on his desk, my lips falling open as a current of desire ripples through me.

"Imagine I'm the man you want," he says. "What am I going to do next?"

"Kiss me," I whisper.

"Where?"

"My lips," I say. "My mouth. Then... My neck."

"Good," he murmurs, his breath skimming along my throat. "Where next?"

Half of me is so embarrassed I want to die, but the other part of me is coming alive, loving this. This is my fantasy.

Everything happens exactly how I want. I don't have to pretend he's someone else. He's the man I want, and he's listening to me tell him exactly what makes me hot.

"And then you push my skirt up," I breathe.

Professor Darius's hands slide up my thighs, his touch sending hot shivers of want straight to my core. I can feel the heat of his body as he steps between them, leaning over me.

"Are you wet?" he whispers into my ear.

Chills rush over my skin, and I lift my hands to him, sliding them around his neck. "Yes."

He takes one of my hands and slides it down my belly, dipping it between my legs. "How wet? Touch yourself."

I'm glad my eyes are closed, because there's no way I could look at him as my fingers caress the wet fabric between my legs.

"Does it feel good?" He asks.

"Yes."

"What should your lover do now?"

"Fuck me," I gasp. I don't know if I'm confessing or instructing, but the words spill out. "Spin me around, bend me over the desk, and fuck me hard."

His stubble rasps against my cheek as his skin caresses mine. "Jade," he whispers.

"Yeah?"

"Pull your panties aside and sink your finger into that wet pussy."

A throb of pleasure runs through me when he pulls back, and I crack my eyes to watch him, his eyes riveted as I draw aside my cotton panties and spread my lips. His breath comes fast as I flick my finger across my swollen clit, then sink lower, finding my opening. Darius's fingers tighten painfully on my knees as he spreads them wider, watching me touch myself.

But it's not enough. I need him, need more.

"Help me," I whisper.

Professor Darius doesn't protest or hesitate. His finger glides in next to mine, pushing mine in deeper. Nothing has touched me here before, not this deep, and a pinch of pain accompanies his deep thrust. I cry out, but pleasure overruns the pain, and the next cry is one of pure bliss. His finger touches places in me I didn't know existed, places that are pure magic. I fall back on my palms, lifting my hips so he can push further. My hair spills down behind me, and my hips rise and fall shamelessly with each thrust of his finger. I don't care what he thinks, I don't care that I have no experience, or that wordless cries of pleasure escape my lips.

I only care about him, and my body, and this magic he's bringing to life inside me when his thumb caresses my clit and he works a second finger into my tightness. When the orgasm comes, it blocks out everything. Only my body exists, my toes curled and my head dropped back, his name echoing in my ears as I cry the words over and over.

*

A knock sounds at my door, and for a second, my heart stops, and I'm sure that I'll open it to find Elowen. But Thorn stands on the other side. Of course it's not Elowen. I accused her of stealing, and now she won't speak to me. She's just on my mind because last time I went to one of these parties, we all got ready together. A pang of regret goes through me, but I try to distract myself by admiring the drop-dead gorgeous man standing in my door wearing a pink shirt unbuttoned at the collar and black dress pants that hug his muscular thighs so well I can't stop staring. His black hair is slicked back, his emerald green eyes are even more piercing than usual, and his chiseled jawline is freshly shaven.

"A man who isn't afraid to wear pink," Asher comments, coming up behind me. "Brave. I like it."

I realize I probably should have said something instead of standing there staring like I've gone mute, but damn. The man takes my breath away.

"Hey," Thorn says, checking me out. My gold dress compliments the golden waves of my hair, which I've given a lot more attention than usual. I'm even wearing heels.

"Hey, yourself," I say, recovering at last.

"I don't mean to rush you, but are you ready?"

"Yeah," I say. "Yeah, sure."

"Did you find your weapon?" he asks.

"No," I say with a sigh. "Unfortunately. Why?"

"No reason," he says. "Your magic just seems a lot more… Manageable."

An inferno of heat rises to my face, and I pray that he somehow doesn't know what that means.

"Well, hopefully that means none of us will do anything stupid tonight," Asher says lightly. "Now, shall we?"

He holds out an elbow, and I slip my hand into it, giving him a grateful smile. For a minute, I pretend I'm the queen of this place, being escorted to a ball by two gorgeous men. And then we reach the bottom of the stairs, where Blonde Bella is standing in the common room in a pink dress that perfectly matches Thorn. I skid to a stop and grab his arm, my eyes wide.

"You must be fucking kidding. Bella is your date?"

He shrugs, avoiding my eyes.

I lower my voice. "You hate Bella."

"I don't *hate* her," he says slowly, looking back and forth between us.

"Since when?"

"Maybe I… Underestimated her," he says. "And why do you care? I thought you liked Rocco."

"I…" Now it's my turn to avert my eyes. I don't know what to say. I did like Rocco. Maybe I still do. But he hurt me. And now Thorn's taking Bella to the ball. He didn't even ask me. I don't know what I expected. None of the guys asked me. They don't like me. I don't know why I can't get it through my head that my attraction to them is not mutual.

"Bella asked me out," he says. "Is there some reason I shouldn't go out with her?"

His gaze is fixed on me so intently that I start squirming. I can wield a knife, but admitting my feelings is a whole other ballgame.

"I thought she was going out with Rocco," I say, grasping at straws. "And it wasn't going to work to make you jealous."

"Well, it worked, didn't it?" Bella says, sliding up beside Thorn and hooking her hand through his elbow. She gives me a smug smile. "Don't worry, I let your other boy-toy down easy. In fact, we're both happier now that we're with the one we truly belong with."

Before I can ask what that means, she turns, steering Thorn away from me.

"Don't stress," Asher says, taking my hand. "You're my date tonight, remember? We're just going to have fun, not hook up."

"I know," I say, shaking my blonde waves back. "Besides, I have someone, just like they do."

"Yeah, you do," Asher says with a grin.

We head out, making our way along the paved pathway through campus to the Great Hall, where the big events like the Unleashing are held. That day, it was full of seats and a platform, but tonight, anything utilitarian has been replaced with glitz and glamour. A red carpet rolls up to the door, with running lights leading us in. Inside, a photo booth overflows with friends taking selfies and photographing each other and their dates.

Bella drags Thorn over to where her other friends are standing—Black-Haired Bella with Ryker, and Brunette Bella with Rocco.

"Oh my God, are you really going to the ball as Asher's *beard?*" Brunette Bella asks, choking back a laugh.

"She thinks she's a sex goddess, but she's really a fag hag," Black-Haired Bella shrieks.

"How's it feel to be stabbed in the back by your best friend?" Blonde Bella sneers. "With a spork!"

They all start howling with laughter. The guys stand there looking uncomfortable. Thorn shoves his hands in his pockets and studies the silver streamers hanging from the ceiling like a thousand glittering icicles. Rocco clears his throat and scratches his cheek. "Let's not worry about anyone else," he says to his date, circling her waist with his muscular arm.

"Leave Jade out of this," Ryker says, steering Bella away from me.

"I'm not even going to think about them tonight," I say, grabbing Asher's hand and dragging him to the dance floor. A slow song is playing, and I wrap my arms around his neck and sway to the music. I never had prom or any of the high school dances, so I'm happy to be here with my friend. Besides, he's as cute as any other guy here. And so what if he's just a friend? I can go to Professor Darius if I need more relief any time I want.

And so, we dance. We dance under the swirling lights and the streamers, to the slow songs and the fast ones. I'm having such a good time I forget all about the guys. That is, until I look over and see two of the Bellas grinding on Rocco, riding his thighs while Ryker and Thorn grind on their asses. Last time I came to one of these, I was the one getting attention. Now, I might as well be invisible. I want to look away, to pretend they're not there, but I can't seem to stop myself. My heart is ripping in two, and I should walk out of here, but I can't stop looking.

The third Bella appears, leaping up onto Rocco. He laughs and catches her, and she wraps her legs around his waist, throws her head back, and starts riding up and down on him.

Suddenly, a scream cuts through the crowd. I yank my eyes away from the orgy spectacle happening and see other students stumbling back. In the center of the floor is a tiny, ugly creature with twisted horns and blazing red eyes.

Well, shit.

Another demonling.

I reach for my knife, only to realize I'm wearing sandals, so I don't have it. The movement catches the creature's eye, though, and it leaps at me. It slams into me, knocking me flat.

"Jade," Asher yells, spinning his nunchucks and knocking the creature off me.

I roll over and grab the creature by the throat and pin it to the floor. "Who's sending you fuckers after me?" I demand.

The demonling begins to squirm, then freezes, its eyes wide. I turn to see Ryker standing over it, his palm extended toward the creature.

"Asher," he says, his gaze never wavering from the monster. "Get Professor Darius. He's in the office."

A minute later, Darius appears, Asher close behind. "Bring the demonling," Darius says to Ryker. "We need to find out how it's getting onto campus."

"Is the party over?" one of the Bellas asks.

"No," Darius says. "Go back to having fun. I'll let you know if anything changes."

Rocco hauls the sturdy little thing up like it weighs nothing, and together we head to the office where they took me after the Unleashing.

"Are you hurt?" Professor Darius asks me, his chocolate eyes searching mine. A throb of excitement flares in my belly as I remember his long fingers stroking my pleasure to unbearable heights.

"I'm fine," I answer, hoping he can't see the blush climbing to my cheeks.

"What the fuck is this thing doing on campus?" Ryker asks, hooking a thumb toward the demonling and glaring daggers. "It's the second one of its kind. Someone is summoning demons to our school."

In that moment, I feel bad for whoever it is, because he looks like he's ready to murder them when he finds out. I hope it's Silas, that scumbag. He deserves it.

"Wake it up," Darius says, bending to peer into the little demon's sickly grey-green face.

Ryker mutters a spell, and a second later, the thing blinks its crusty eyes.

"Why are you here?" I demand when it begins to squirm in Rocco's grip.

"Summoned," the demonling chatters in a surprisingly high, whiny voice.

"We know that," Ryker says.

"D-don't hurt me," the demonling stutters. "Was only doing job."

"For who?" I ask.

"I know no names," it says in its same sniveling voice.

"And you were summoned to kill me?" I ask.

"N-no," it protests. "No killing. This demonling do only odd jobs."

I narrow my eyes, checking the reactions of the sorcerers. They look convinced, but I'm not buying it.

"You attacked me," I say. "And one of your kind attacked me a few months ago. Someone must be sending you."

"Demonlings can't lie," Professor Darius murmurs, his hand grazing my back.

"Why are you here?" Ryker asks.

"Unlock magical item," it stammers. "Channel energy."

I straighten, seeing the understanding dawn in the eyes of the sorcerer's at the same time I realize it. "My spork," I say. "Someone here has Cleo."

The demonling nods vigorously. "I never hurt humans," it says. "Don't hurt me."

I still don't know if I believe it, but Professor Darius nods. "We won't hurt you. You've been a great help. Can you tell us anything about the person? What they look like? Where you went?"

"I go where summoned," the demonling says. "All humans, they look alike."

"Well, that's just super," I say, flopping into a chair. "Someone here has Cleo, but we can't find them. And finals are coming next week, which means my magic will be at one level through the whole thing. How can I control that?"

Professor Darius puts a hand on my shoulder. "We'll get you through this, Jade. We'll find a way."

"And what if you can't?" I ask, looking up at him. "What if I fail my finals?"

Because everyone knows what happens to people who get kicked out of the Academy of Sorcery. You get assigned a job working for someone powerful who can siphon off your magic and use it for themselves so that you can't hurt anyone with it. Since I already work for someone powerful who owns my contract for the next three decades, he'd definitely be the first person the Society of Supernaturals looks at if I flunk out of the Academy, which I'm sure to do without Cleo. And considering my magic and Silas's morals, it looks like I'm about to start my career as a magical prostitute.

"It's the Bellas," I blurt out, unable to hold myself back. "It has to be them. That's why they're suddenly getting all this—male attention." I finish speaking and wish I could swallow my words, take them back and say them when I'm alone with Darius. Now it looks like I'm this jealous fool, accusing the girls who took the attention of the hottest guys on campus away from me. Basically, I sound like a pathetic, jealous hag.

"You think we're enchanted?" Ryker asks, fixing me with that glare that I was just pitying the recipient of.

"Don't you think it's funny that none of you liked them, and suddenly you're all dating them?"

Neither of the guys answer. Ryker gives me a stormy glare, and Rocco crosses his arms and frowns at the floor.

"Thorn," Professor Darius says.

The door cracks open, and Thorn sticks his head in from his position guarding the door. "Yes, Professor?"

"I want the Bellas' rooms searched for Jade's weapon," he says. "Take Jade with you."

I gape, shocked that he's going along with my hunch, since I have nothing to go on. And there's a little bit of guilt, too, because I'm not entirely convinced they're to blame for the theft. But if there's even a chance, then I have to take it. Not just to get my spork back, but to keep my magic from doing exactly what I said I would never do with it—seduce a guy against his will. Maybe I'm not the one doing it, but I'm not about to let someone else use my magic for evil, either. If that's what's going on, I have to put an end to it. I have to save my guys.

James & Phoenix

Chapter 21

"It has to be here," I say, now feeling as desperate as I sound. I've convinced myself I can feel my magic up here in their dorm rooms, but after two rooms, we've found nothing.

"Want to strip search me, dyke?" Blonde Bella asks, sneering at me. The other two are standing against the wall in the hall, glaring like they want me dead.

"I'll leave the strip searching to your boyfriend," I say, shooting a resentful glance at Thorn.

"I'm not her boyfriend," he mutters, lifting up Bella's mattress. They've already used their magic to search the room, but they're now searching by hand, since the spork has so many spells protecting her from detection.

Bella looks unconcerned about his denial. "Give me time," she says with a smug smile.

At last, the guys come out of her room, as empty-handed as they were after the others. And now I've really pissed off the Bellas. If they only made fun of me before, now they hate me. Now they have a real reason to. And they'll probably spread it all around campus, how I'm so jealous that I accused them and had their rooms torn apart because I can't handle the fact that they got the guys and I didn't.

I lean against the wall and close my eyes, massaging my temples.

"Let me walk you home."

I open my eyes, surprised to find Rocco standing in front of me, only sympathy in his eyes.

I sigh. "Okay."

"Don't take too long," Brunette Bella sings out, waving her fingers at Rocco. "I'll be waiting."

"Ugh," I mutter, stomping down the hall. There's really no reason Rocco needs to escort me to the next floor, but he falls into step beside me anyway.

"I'm sorry your spork is still missing," he says.

I search for the joke in his eyes, but no smartass comment comes. "Thanks," I mumbled, starting up the stairs.

"Do you want us to search that necromancer's room?"

I think of how hurt Elowen was when I accused her, and I can't bear the thought of hurting her more. I can only hope she's doing okay and has made new friends. "No," I say with a sigh. "I don't think she'd take it."

"You know, you have the magic," Rocco says. "You're the one with the power. That's what matters."

"Is it?" I ask, stopping outside my room. "Because it doesn't feel like it." I want to add that it doesn't matter since he's still going home with Bella, but I stop myself. I'm being a jealous bitch. They don't have my spork. I saw it proven with my own eyes. Suddenly, all I want to do is sink into a warm bubble bath and forget this night ever happened.

"Whoever stole it, they might be using up what you stored in there, but you're making more all the time," Rocco says. "You have that power naturally, Jade. They don't. All they have is a stolen item that'll be useless once you're not supplying it."

"An item I need," I say with a sigh. "But thanks for trying to make me feel better. I appreciate it."

"I… I'm sorry I couldn't handle it," he says, avoiding my eyes. "Your magic. It's too much for me."

"It's okay," I say, unlocking my room and stepping inside. "Don't feel bad, Rocco. It's water under the bridge. You found someone you can handle, and I found someone who can handle me."

His gaze snaps to mine, and his nostrils flare. "What? You did?"

I know I shouldn't, but I smile at the flash of jealousy in him. "Goodnight, Rocco," I say through the crack in my door, then pull it closed. Somehow, I feel better knowing that he's jealous, too.

*

All too soon, finals arrive. Since we couldn't find Cleo, I turned my focus to training with Asher every spare second for the week leading up to the magical trials. It's kinda nice to throw myself completely into something, not thinking about the gossip on campus about my accusation, or how much I miss Elowen and the guys. Our relationship might have started contentiously, but after a while, I got used to them. At least I still have Asher, because even Ryker seems uninterested in pushing me past my limits every day in swordplay, as if he's given up on my future at the academy and realizes that making me better is a waste of time.

So, I focus on my finals. I may not have Cleo, but I'm not going down without a fight. If they boot me from the Academy, they're going to have to drag me out kicking and screaming.

When the day arrives, I'm so nervous I can't eat. As we reach the Great Hall, where we have to pass a series of trials as our finals, I stop Asher. I'm so nervous I'm shaking, but I'm as ready as I can be without Cleo.

"Hey, in case I don't pass, will you go see Elowen and make sure she's okay?" I ask. "I tried to text her wishing her luck, but she blocked me on her phone, and the House of Necromancy wouldn't let me in to see her."

"Girl, shut up," Asher says. "You're going to pass and tell her yourself."

"Thanks for the vote of confidence," I say. "But we both know I'm already getting a zero on my test for passing magic to my object. And anything else that takes finesse. I'll just be blasting everything I have at each challenge."

"Magic is magic," he says. "That's what they tell us in Wizardry class. You can focus it to do whatever you want. Yours just naturally comes out a certain way. You can change that, remember?"

"Yes," I say, wiping my hands on my uniform skirt. "But you know it's unlikely that I'll pass. So just shut up and let me say this."

Asher looks like he'll protest again, but then he nods. "What's up?"

"I just wanted to say that you're the best friend I've ever had," I say. "You saved me from that demonling."

"You would have thrown it off," Asher says with a shrug. "I just helped."

"And you saved me from myself more times than I can count," I say. "I would have beaten the Bellas asses so many times if not for you."

"Hey, I was just trying to keep you from getting kicked out," he says. "So let's go keep that from happening today. Ready, partner?"

"Ready," I say, grinning at him. I am ready. Now that I've gotten the mushy stuff out of the way, I'm ready to kick ass.

Inside, we find our way to the floor. Our first challenge is to ignore distractions while levitating and holding the weight of our partner. We wait our turn, watching most students pass with flying colors while a few fail and run after the distraction. Finally, it's our turn. Professor Darius is standing aside, along with a few other instructors, grading each pair.

"Ready?" Darius asks, his reassuring gaze finding mine.

I nod, nerves tying my stomach in knots.

"You have plenty of magic, Jade," he says. "Just concentrate and focus. Don't let the distractions disrupt your train of thought. You should do fine."

I nod, then head out onto the floor with my partner in crime. Eyes closed, I focus on my body becoming light as air, trying to concentrate enough to rise from the ground. Using my wand, I channel magic into it, say an incantation to levitate.

Suddenly, a familiar voice cuts through my concentration— one I missed so much that tears spring to my eyes. *Mom.*

I know it's a distraction, an illusion to distract me, but it's all I can do not to turn to her. It sounds so real, as if she's standing right there. I'd give anything to see her one more time.

But it's not real. I know it's not. My hands are shaking in Asher's as I try to tune out my mother's voice calling my name. A voice I thought I'd never hear again, saying my name with such anguish I can hardly bear it. Tears stream down my face as I squeeze my eyes shut, trying desperately to push it away.

I feel sweat misting my forehead as I try to stay focused on Asher, gripping his hands while I whisper the chant again and again, trying to rise from the floor. Forcing the room to go quiet in my mind, everything fades away but the image of me and Asher rising into the air, high enough to prove I can control my magic despite distractions. At last, I repeat the words we learned in class to lower us both, and we slowly float back to the floor.

I open my eyes and let out a cheer, pumping my fist in the air. "I did it!"

"Yeah, you did," Asher says, grinning back at me.

"Your turn," I say, confident that Asher can do anything I can do. He closes his eyes and recites the chant, and a second later, we begin to rise. He must hear something too, though, because suddenly he jerks around, and our feet thud back to the floor. I grip his hands tighter when he tries to start for the door. I yank him back and force him to meet my gaze. "Focus, Asher," I say in an even voice. "It's not real. I heard it, too. It's an illusion to distract us. They told us that would happen, remember?"

"Right, sorry," he says, licking his lips and closing his eyes again.

After three or four minutes, he's back in his groove, and he's able to levitate with me, hover, and lower us back to the floor.

When we're back on solid ground, Asher lets out a sigh and gives me a quick hug. "Thanks for having my back, girl," he says. "It was so real…"

"I know," I say, wiping my face to make sure my earlier tears are gone. "But we both passed that challenge. Ready for combat?"

Asher goes first, and I watch as he does his thing, kicking his opponent's ass using nothing but magic and his nunchucks. I'm there to cheer him on and for moral support, but my stomach is in knots. Without my weapon, I have to use a non-magical sparring sword, and my chances are slim at best. At least I have some skill, and I've practiced until I can do it by muscle memory alone. But I can't beat someone who can draw strength from their magic.

While sitting on the sidelines trying to psych myself up for my final so I don't completely lose it, a slight figure scurries over, a hood pulled low over her face. My mind immediately flashes back to the beautiful woman who attacked me before.

"Oh, fuck no," I say, grabbing my knife from my boot.

"Jade, it's me," an urgent whisper hisses from inside the hood.

"Elowen?" I ask, confused.

She peeks out of her hood, checking the people on either side of us before leaning in closer. "I'm not supposed to be here," she whispers. "They'd think I was messing up the light magic trials."

"Oh my god, I'm so sorry I accused you," I say, grabbing her hands in mine. "I've been trying to call you for weeks."

"Don't apologize," she says, her brown eyes filling with tears. "I don't deserve it. But I had to come. I can't let you go down like this."

Suddenly, I can't breathe. "What?"

"I…I stole your spork," she blurts out, a tear rolling down her cheek.

Now I know why they call it a knife in the back. Because her betrayal feels like one. "Why?" I ask, my voice shaking.

"She forced me to," Elowen cries. "She said if I didn't, she'd get me expelled."

"Who?"

"Bella, of course," she says. "Her parents are in the Society of Supernaturals. They can do anything they want. And if I got thrown out and had to go to work for someone who wanted to use my dark magic for evil…" She shudders, more tears falling from her eyes.

I'm reminded about my own situation and how easily the crooked judge gave our lives to Silas. "Okay, I get it," I say. "But you need to give it back."

I feel sorry for her, but I'm pissed, too.

"I don't have it," she says. "I gave it to Bella. She couldn't get the magic out of it, so she's been summoning demons to do it."

"Why?" I demand.

"So she could make Thorn fall in love with her, of course," Elowen says. "And maybe to make you fail."

She sniffles and wipes her nose.

"We searched her room," I say. "All their rooms. They didn't have it."

"She made me keep it in my room when she wasn't using it," Elowen chokes out. "She tried to get me to use it, too, but I wouldn't. I promise I never touched your magic."

"Actually, you did," I say, my fists balling tighter and tighter. "When you took Cleo."

"I didn't use it," Elowen sobs. "I told her yesterday that I wouldn't hide it for her anymore, and I gave it back. She's going to get me kicked out now. I had to tell you before I go. I'm so sorry, Jade. I was just so scared."

"You should have come to me," I say. "I'm your friend. You could have trusted me the way I trusted you."

"I know," Elowen says, her shoulders shaking with sobs. "I'm so sorry, Jade. I told you I wasn't good."

I'm too mad to forgive her yet, or even talk to her. I defended her to everyone. I trusted her, and I was wrong. If I had let Rocco search her room the first day she stole it, I'd have had it all along. But I put my friends above what was right in front of my face. I didn't believe it because I didn't want to believe it. I wanted to believe we all have a choice, that we are more than our magic. I wanted to believe she could be good despite her magic just like I wanted to believe my life wouldn't be ruled by mine. Maybe I was wrong about all of it. Maybe I'm my magic, and she is hers. Maybe we don't get to choose.

"I better go find my weapon before I fail the next two trials and get kicked out of school," I say. "You're not the only one with that worry."

She lets out a little sob, and I feel like shit for being a bitch to her. But she stole from me.

"Thanks for telling me," I say. "I'll find you later, and we'll talk about this."

"Bella Goodwin has it," she chokes out, doubling over to cover her face.

Pushing my way through the students in line, I find Blonde Bella. It's time to confront her. "So, I hear you have something that belongs to me."

Bella just stares at me, all perfect skin and innocence. "What are you talking about?"

"Admit it," I say. "Or we can do this the hard way."

Bella crosses her arms and smirks at me. "Girls, look," she purrs. "Dumpster's finally losing it."

"Hard way it is," I say. "I've been dying to put you in your place."

I pull back my fist and punch her in the face.

Bella screams and collapses to the floor.

But I don't just want to send a message, I want to start a war. So I jump onto her, punching her again. She hits back, boxing me in the ear. I throw another jab, and she bucks, rolling us over. While Bella and I roll around on the floor, beating the crap out of each other, everyone gathers around, yelling and cheering us on. Adrenaline races through me, addictive and empowering. The three sorcery students, Asher, and Elowen are in the crowd. I can almost hear them rooting for me to give Bella the ass kicking she deserves.

After a few minutes, I wear Bella down and pin her to the floor. "Where's my spork?"

Bella lifts her head off the floor and spits, barely missing my face. Fortunately, I have faster reflexes. I pull back my fist, about to hit her again, but someone grabs me and drags me off her.

"What the hell is going on?" Professor Darius demands. He stares at his sorcery students. "And why didn't any of you stop it?"

The three boys seem to shake out of a trance. "It happened so fast," Rocco says, scratching the back of his neck.

"Jade and Bella," Darius says. "In my office. Now."

We follow the professor back to the office which is becoming all too familiar. Bella flounces in, hand over her nose, blood seeping between her fingers.

"If you broke my nose, and it heals crooked, my daddy will make you pay," she hisses.

Her parents are powerful enough that Elowen caved and stole from me because of that threat. I won't cower to that kind of bully, though. I have nothing to lose. My life already belongs to a conniving asshole. She can't make my future worse than it'll be if I don't get Cleo back, and I fail out of the Academy.

Darius hands Bella a box of tissues that she uses to clean her bloody nose. Then he sits across from us, hands on his desk. "I realize you two haven't hit it off, but this has gotten out of hand. What's going on?"

"She has Cleo," I say. "Elowen told me."

Bella glares at me. "Jade's just jealous that Thorn likes me better."

"Is that true?" Darius asks, his eyes searching mine. My heart squeezes when I find hurt in his gaze.

"What does that have to do with anything?" I ask, widening my eyes. "She coerced my friend into stealing my spork, then summoned demonlings to campus to siphon the magic to use for herself. *My* magic."

Darius gives his head a quick shake. "You're right. The rest is irrelevant."

"I had to," Bella wails. "She gets to be around him all the time. I barely even see him!"

I turn to her, my jaw dropping in disbelief. "Are you really so desperate for a guy that you'd steal my magic to get him?"

"It worked, didn't it?" she snaps.

"Yeah, but he doesn't actually like you," I point out. "You might as well get him drunk and take advantage of him."

"Don't you think I've tried that?"

"Oh my god," I say, turning back to Darius. "Do you hear her? I thought she was this powerful witch, but she's just a sad little bitch who can't think about anything but whether a guy wants her."

"You better watch who you're calling a bitch," Bella says, starting to rise from her chair.

"Sit," Darius barks, holding up a hand.

Bella falls back into her chair and glares at him, her arms crossed over her chest.

"I'm sorry to say this, but I'm afraid we may have to expel you," Darius says to her. "We try not to ever expel students, but tampering with someone's magic is a serious offense."

"What?" Bella shrieks. "You can't expel me. You don't understand how much pressure I'm under from my parents. They'll kill me if I'm expelled!"

"Maybe you should have thought of that before leaving me with a huge handicap for half this semester," I snap.

"I'm sorry." She breaks down into hiccupping sobs, covering her face with both hands. "Don't kick me out. I can't be someone's servant."

Oh, the nerve of this bitch. After making fun of me for being someone's servant all semester, now she's got a glimpse of what that life is like, and she's blubbering like a baby.

Still, the reality of what she's about to face makes my blood run cold and my spine stiffen. I wouldn't wish a contract like mine on my worst enemy. "Give me my weapon," I say quietly.

Bella pulls it from her pocket and hands me Cleo. The moment she's in my hand, our connection seems to snap taut, and for the first time in weeks I feel like I can really breathe. I hold her to my chest and stare at Bella.

"Don't look at me. I'm ugly when I cry," she chokes out through her sobs.

"That's really it, isn't it?" I say. "You have nothing but your looks, and they didn't work, so you had to resort to this. You really have nothing in your life except a giant hole that you think Thorn can fill."

"I'll tell," she hisses, her wild eyes flying between me and Darius. "I'll tell Headmaster Orville about you two."

Professor Darius freezes.

"Tell them what, exactly?" I ask. "He's my teacher. There's nothing going on."

Bella gives me a smug smile. "No? Well, they don't have to know that. You get private lessons with Professor Darius. Who knows what goes on behind closed doors."

"Tell you what," I say, realizing I better fix this. There are telepaths here who could figure out what happened between me and Darius in minutes. "I'm not going to press charges, or file a report, or whatever the procedure is at the Academy. I'll even forgive you for stealing my magic and my vessel, because I feel sorry for you."

"What?" she asks, narrowing her eyes. She's wrong about her beauty. Even with a splotchy, tear-stained face, she's still pretty. But no matter how beautiful she is, how much makeup she puts on or how much magic she steals, she can't change the fact that deep inside, she's an ugly, mean little person.

"That's right," I say, standing and squaring my shoulders. "I won't have you punished, but you owe me one. And rest assured, I will collect."

"Are you sure about this, Jade?" Professor Darius asks.

"Let her stay," I say. "But she also needs to call off the demonlings and that dark magic lady who attacks me every time I leave campus."

"I'll uninvite the demonlings to campus, but I don't know what lady you're talking about."

"Someone very powerful came after Jade and the other sorcerers several times," Professor Darius says, fixing Bella with a hard stare.

She cowers, visibly shaking, her eyes wide. "It wasn't me. I swear it!"

"I'm done here," I say. "Leave me the fuck alone until I come to collect my favor. Now, if you'll excuse me, I have a final to ace."

"Go ahead," Darius says, gesturing to the door. He gives me a smile that makes my heart flip and adds, "Good luck."

I return to the Great Hall to complete the next trial. Cleo is practically singing in my hand, and I can't believe I ever doubted her. I don't think I'll ever put her down again. She feels like part of me, an extension of my arm. I pour magic into her, and the relief is instant and overwhelming.

"I'm sorry," I whisper to her. "I treated you like shit, but I'll never do it again."

"Jade?" Ryker says, coming over to join me. "Ready?"

"Fuck yeah," I say. "And I'm going to kick your ass this time."

I step onto the floor, the magic humming between me and Cleo. After using a dummy sword for so long, I could laugh out loud at how alive my weapon feels in my hand now. I barely know I've given the command before a long, beautiful gleaming sword shimmers in my hand.

"Thanks, girl," I whisper, circling Ryker.

He knocked me to the floor too many times this semester. Now it's my turn. We parry a few times, and then I feint to the left. When he moves to attack, I lunge in and strike. Ryker stumbles back and falls to the floor. I leap forward, positioning the tip of my sword at his throat like he's done a hundred times in swordsmanship class.

"Pinned ya," I say with a grin.

For the first time in maybe his entire life, Ryker grins back. "Congratulations," he says, knocking my sword away and jumping to his feet. He holds out a hand to shake mine. "You passed."

I'm so excited I throw my arms around him and squeeze him as hard as I can. Ryker looks so startled I can't help but laugh.

"I did it," I crow. "I fucking did it!"

"Yeah, you fucking did," he says, smiling down at me, one arm still around my waist. His gaze dips to my lips, and my breath catches. And I *want*.

Ryker steps back from me, and I try to shake off the feeling. My head is spinning. I couldn't afford to release any magic while finals were coming up, but now that I've put plenty into Cleo, I know that's not the problem. The problem is that I can't resist him, bastard or not. And I can't read minds, but I'm pretty sure the feeling is mutual.

He clears his throat and gestures toward the door with his sword. "Ready for your third trial?"

"The final final," I say, trying to make a joke though my pulse is racing at the thought.

Ryker doesn't crack a smile this time. "Let's go."

"Guess I'm as ready as I'm going to get," I mutter, following him out of the Great Hall and toward the last test, the one that determines whether or not I'll stay at the Academy of Sorcery.

Chapter 22

"Considering you've not had time to practice with your weapon, you will do yours outside, away from any other students who could be injured," Darius explains to me as we head out. The final challenge involves gathering all the magic we possess and focusing it intently, then transferring it back and forth with our vessel until we recognize the right balance within ourselves that won't endanger anyone but gives us plenty of magic to work with.

"To prevent injuries, or unintended orgies?" I ask, flashing a grin at Darius.

"Yes, that is a concern," he acknowledges with a small smile, looking unruffled by my comment. He holds the door open for me, and then the three sorcery students and I follow him to a small group of palm trees behind the Great Hall. Under them, a patch of scruffy grass surrounded by palmettos gives us some privacy from anyone leaving their final.

"This looks like a good spot," Darius says. "I know you haven't gotten to practice gathering magic into yourself much, since you've been trying to regulate it without conventional means."

He gives me a meaningful look, and I feel heat rising to my cheeks. I catch Thorn's scowl, and the look in his eyes says he's guessed exactly how I regulated my magic.

Crap.

If he turns Darius in to the headmaster…

"Stand in the middle and prepare your weapon," Darius says, oblivious to the resentful look being cast his way.

"Focus, Jade," I whisper under my breath. They can work out their issues later. I need to harness all the magic I can and get it to Cleo right now.

I pull out my spork and hold her up in front of me like she's the fucking sword of King Arthur, my little three-tined Excalibur. I dare anyone to laugh at her unimpressive disguise. I know what she can do.

Holding her aloft, I begin to move my magic back and forth, letting it flow as if she's a part of me, which is how she feels today. Even with Professor Darius's private lessons, it's never been this easy. I wonder if she missed me as much as I missed her. After a few minutes, I glance over and notice the guys looking uncomfortable.

I'm starting to squirm myself. It's one thing to focus my magic, to turn it to levitating. It's another just to handle it raw, not changing it or focusing it to do my bidding.

My eyes meet Rocco's, and I remember his mouth on me, his tongue forcing into my virgin opening, and my knees clench together. Rocco scratches the back of his neck and shuffles a few steps toward me. Fuck. Can he read my mind?

"Jade," he says. "I... I'm sorry. I don't know what was wrong with me. Just that, I guess when they had your magic, I recognized it somehow, subconsciously. I was drawn to them because they had stolen a part of *you*."

"You were sleeping with Bella because she reminded you of me?"

He rubs the back of his head again. "Well... Yeah. I know it sounds lame. But that's what happened."

My damn magic. Not only did it let them seduce my guys, but it let them somehow feel familiar to the guys, feel like me. I suddenly wish I hadn't spared Bella a cruel fate.

Professor Darius clears his throat. "Rocco," he says quietly. "Let Jade focus."

Rocco casts a glance their way, his brows lifted like he'd forgotten they were there. "Right. Sorry, Jade."

He slips back into place with the others, leaving me in the center of the clearing. Standing here holding my sword, I suddenly feel very powerful. Sexy. More than that, I feel an aching need inside me, ravenous and unquenchable. I lock eyes with Thorn, summoning him to me like I did in the club. He shifts and glances to either side, like they can help him. But the other sorcerers are staring at me with the same glazed looks they gave me when I was rolling around with Bella.

This time, I don't have to share the attention.

Thorn takes a tentative step toward me, and I bite my lower lip, my body humming with desire for him. I don't care if it's the magic or not. I just want him. It really is like being intoxicated. It lets me do what I wouldn't be brave enough to do otherwise.

Thorn stops in front of me, his hands balled into fists.

"What's your excuse?" I ask.

"I didn't sleep with Bella," he says. "She wanted to, but I... Didn't."

I can't stand the separation of our bodies any longer. I step to him, closing the distance between us, and wrap my arms around his neck. The sensation of our bodies colliding knocks the breath out of me. "Kiss me," I say, imploring him with my gaze.

Thorn's arms tighten around me, and his mouth dips to mine. His lips are soft but sure against mine, and I melt into the kiss, feeling his strong arms around me and his hard body pressing relentlessly against mine. His tongue slides between my lips, caressing mine, deepening the kiss. When he pulls away, his hands slide down my back, his mouth dipping to my neck, sending chills through my entire body.

Over his shoulder, I catch sight of our audience. Instead of feeling embarrassed that I'd forgotten them, a thrill races through me, and my thighs dampen with lust. Before I can think better of it, I motion for them to join us. Ryker and Rocco don't hesitate. Obeying my command, they press in next to me.

Ryker stands behind me, tugging my chin around to kiss me the way he did in the studio that day. His lips are insatiable, his kiss mouthwatering. Thorn's lips tug at my skin, kissing my neck harder, while Rocco's breath heats my shoulder and his hands stroke my body, pinching my nipple until I whimper into Ryker's mouth. His cock throbs against my ass at the sound, and wetness pools between my legs.

Somehow, impossibly, I want more. My body is on fire, overwhelmed by pleasure, but it's not enough. I'm like an addict needing a fix.

"Darius," I gasp, pulling away from the kiss to welcome him. But he just gives a short shake of his head, his jaw clenched and his eyes clouded with lust. Somehow, he can resist, but it doesn't bother me. I'm glad the others have given in, even if he hasn't. I think I'd die if they weren't touching me, kissing me, exploring me.

Rocco plants his lips on mine, and I respond hungrily, eager to taste his mouth. His hand slips between the buttons of my shirt, teasing the edge of my full breast until I am squirming for more, my nipple so hard it hurts, begging for his touch. Thorn starts unbuttoning my shirt for him, and I arch my back in pleasure, letting my breasts rise toward them. Thorn makes quick work of my shirt, spreading it open and peeling down the cup of my bra to take my nipple in his mouth.

I let out a muffled cry as Thorn's mouth closes around my nipple, his tongue caressing it while Rocco's tongue plunges into my mouth. Ryker's hand slides down my belly and under my skirt. Rocco finds my other nipple and begins to tweak and tug at it while Thorn strokes the other with his tongue. I arch back again, hooking an arm around Ryker's neck and grinding my ass against his hard length. He rocks against me, dipping his hand between my thighs.

Nudging them apart, he slips his fingers into my wetness. I whimper with pleasure, my knees going weak. Thorn supports my weight, spreading my knees for Ryker's probing fingers. He sinks a finger deep inside me, and I moan with pleasure. Their hands knead and caress, their tongues stroking me to greater heights each moment. Rocco's hand drags up my thigh, pulling my skirt with it. He tugs my panties aside and circles my clit with his finger while Ryker keeps thrusting his finger into me. Rocco slicks over my swollen nub until I can hardly stand it.

Then he slides lower, sinking his finger into me at the same time as his brother.

"Fuck, you're so tight," he groans, his mouth hot against my neck.

The pleasure ripples through me, and I can hardly breathe. I drop my head back against Ryker's shoulder as Thorn's hand joins theirs, coating his fingers in my juices as he explores my folds and teases my clit until I'm writhing against him. He starts to press against my opening, and I cry out in pleasure and pain as he stretches me open further, his finger joining the other two. They drive into me together, in a maddening rhythm until I can't bear it another second. A cry tears from my lips, and white flashes behind my eyelids as a climax grips every inch of my body. Their fingers continue pumping deeper into me, slippery and hot, as I ride the waves of pleasure until I'm nothing but a quivering puddle of satisfaction.

When I open my eyes, I have to blink to believe my eyes. The trees are as green as if we've had months of rain and warmth, as if it is April instead of December. The grass underfoot is deep and bright, with flowers dotting the lush green carpet. Butterflies burst from cocoons and flit over the flowers.

"I must admit, I'm impressed," a silky, feminine voice cuts in just as a blasting wind begins to blow. I'm jerked from my afterglow, and I spin around, expecting one of the Bellas. Instead, I find the beautiful enchantress who attacked me outside my father's house.

The guys jump away from me, snatching for their weapons. I don't know what happened to Cleo during our tryst, but she's in my hand now, humming with power. I can feel her eagerness to fight, to impale this bitch, as clearly as if she were speaking words into my mind.

"Who are you?" Rocco demands. The woman stands in front of something that looks like a slash in the fabric of the universe—a long, vertical tear that she must have stepped through. All I can see through it is an endless void of darkness. It seems to have some kind of magnetic pull, like a black hole, because all around us, the trees are twisting, boughs straining toward the opening. Leaves and twigs break free and are sucked into the vacuum, along with the new butterflies with their crinkled wings and the petals of the delicate flowers.

That's when I see Darius. He drops to one knee and bows his head, his voice reverent as he breathes, "Lilith."

"I see that someone remembers me," she says with a huff, her hair whipping around her face and blowing out behind her in dark streams. "This is what happens when men rule the world. The memorable women are forgotten."

"What the hell is going on?" I ask, not sure whether to bow or attack.

"I'm not the villain here," Lilith says. "I'm not the devil's whore or the queen of sin. I'm simply the queen of the spirit world." Her eyes dazzle, their power incredible and intimidating.

"Got it," I say, eyeing the opening behind her. If that's the spirit world, I want no part of it. It sucks in a branch and a palm frond like a hungry mouth.

"These sorcerers, as powerful as they are, cannot teach you what you need to know to take your place as the High Priestess when the time comes."

"I think I made myself clear the last time you asked," I snap, holding Cleo toward her, my own hair snapping and whipping around me, sucked toward the doorway.

Lilith lets out a tinkle of laughter. "My dear, weapons will not work on me. I'm immortal. Even a sword wielded by the High Priestess won't injure me. Send me back to the spirit realm, maybe. I cannot be killed."

"What do you want?" I ask, tossing my hair out of my face.

"If you truly want to learn how to control your powers, you must come with me. A priestess's magic is neither light nor dark, but a balance of both. Only I can teach you what it truly means to the High Priestess. I am the original High Priestess, the one who bestows my powers upon a living soul. I hope you will consider my offer." She smiles and spreads her arms wide, power radiating from her hands and shooting into the sky. "Our powers are more persuasive than even force."

I feel a strong pull to Lilith, as if a gravitational force is leading me to follow her, pulling on me the way the doorway behind her is tugging on the world around us.

I step toward her, my feet moving of their own accord. The wind helps me along, drawing me closer and closer to this woman who wants me so much.

Before I reach her, Ryker leaps in front of me. "Lilith will take you into the land of the dead, but you need to learn light magic first. Otherwise the dark could take over within you."

Lilith smiles at Ryker, and he stumbles, his eyes confused and unfocused, then drops to his knees. He looks up at her with those same blank, dazed eyes. "My queen," he says.

Seeing him act like a puppet breaks my own trance. "Let him go," I yell, slicing through the relentless wind with my blade.

"If you come with me, I will gladly leave your admirers in peace." Lilith steps closer, reaching for my wrist. "Come with me to the spirit world, child."

My own resistance crumbles the moment her cool fingers close around my wrist. The wind ceases to tear at me, though it still blows without stopping around us. Suddenly, I know that everything will be well if I go with her. Some intrinsic force is urging me toward her, and I know it's right. The spirit world is where I belong. Lilith is who I belong with, who I belong to. My feet lead me forward, and a deep peace settles over me as I follow the raven-haired beauty to the doorway. It no longer looks ominous. Now that I see clearly, it looks dark and peaceful as sleep.

Term 1: Unleashing Trials

I step forward, but before I can step through, Darius knocks me to the ground, lifts his hand high, and plunges his snake staff into Lilith.

Chapter 23

When the snake's head sinks into Lilith, something shatters inside me, and I scream. "No!"

Lilith tumbles into the doorway, and it shimmers violently before sealing shut with a wrenching wind and a burst of black smoke. I fall forward onto hands and knees, clawing at the air and choking on the smoke as the wind ceases, and the world around us falls silent.

"Jade," Thorn says, falling to his knees beside me. He wraps his arms around me, hauling me up and into his lap.

"Are you hurt?" Darius asks, crouching beside us.

I slowly blink away the trance that came over me. I can't explain the twisting feeling inside me, but it's almost as if I could feel the cane impaling Lilith.

The only thing I can think to say is, "What... The... Actual... Fuck."

"Exactly what I was thinking," Rocco says with a halfhearted smile.

Ryker stalks away to inspect some vibrant greenery.

My gaze wanders from one man to the next, finally stopping on Darius. "Did you kill her?"

He grimaces. "She can't be killed. She's been around as long as the devil himself."

"Okay," I say, rubbing my temples. "And it's probably safe to say she'll be back?"

"I have no doubt."

"Super," I mutter, then take a deep breath and shake my hair back. Part of me wants to stand, but I feel too safe in Thorn's arms right now, and I need that a little longer. "So, tell me what you know about this lady. I need to know what I'm up against."

"Legend has it that Lilith was the first woman, created for Adam. She refused to be subservient to anyone, even Adam, so she was thrown into hell. God made a new woman for Adam— Eve. That's about the gist of it. She's extremely powerful, maybe even more so than Lucifer himself."

"What does she want with me?"

"It must be your magic. Jade, your magic is the energy of life itself, the power of all creation. Look around you. Look what you did."

I glance around at the butterflies dancing over blooms that burst to life in the middle of December. I saw them, and in some way I must have known it was me, but I didn't really think about it until this moment. I made a mini-spring occur in minutes. I brought things back to life. Maybe even brought them into existence in the first place.

Okay, I can see how the powers that be might feel threatened by that. After all, weren't the gods supposed to be in charge of creation?

Suddenly, a cold knot drops into my belly. "What if she goes after my dad?"

"We'll put another ward in place on his house just in case," Darius says.

"Good thing he never leaves the house," I say, my voice trembling slightly.

Thorn's arms tighten around me.

"You're safe," he murmurs.

"I know the last few months have been hard," Darius says, smoothing my hair. "But I promise we won't let anything happen to you."

I sigh and lean my head against his hand. He's been my comfort these last few months—my only comfort.

"Let's get you back to your room," Thorn murmurs in my ear. I nod, climbing off his lap with some reluctance.

As we start back toward the dorm, Ryker's eye catches mine. I see longing there, but also pain as he looks between me and the others. "I should go check on the trials," he says.

"Come with us," I implore him, offering a tentative smile.

His lips press together for a second, and then he shakes his head. "You have three guards. You don't need me." Before I can say otherwise, he turns and strides off toward the Great Hall.

I can see the tension in his shoulders, and a part of me wants to run after him, to tell him that I do need him.

"Give him time," Rocco says, resting a gentle hand on my lower back. "He'll come around. He's been through a lot, Jade. You have to be patient with him."

"What do you mean?" I ask. "What's he been through?"

"That's not my place to tell," Rocco says. "When he's ready to share that, he will."

"How can I understand him if he won't tell me?"

Rocco shakes his head. "Patience, Cinderella."

"You're not supposed to call me that anymore."

"Actually, I think I won that bet," he says with a grin. "You ready to pay up?"

I gulp at the memory of what I promised him. "Can we take a rain check on that?"

He laughs and throws an arm around me. "Whenever you're ready," he says. "But you're just postponing the inevitable."

"I am, huh?" I ask, giving him a saucy smile.

"Face it, we're gonna fuck," he says. "It was always gonna happen. It's just a matter of when."

I check over my shoulder, glad to see that Thorn and Darius are deep in conversation and appear not to have heard that. We arrive back at the dorm too soon. I'm not ready to be alone, and apparently no one else is, either. Everyone is in the common room, celebrating the end of the term and recounting their most harrowing and hilarious trials from the day. No one pays us any mind as we head upstairs to my room.

"Sure you don't want to cash in that rain check right now?" Rocco asks with a wink.

"I thought you had Bella for that," I tease, trying to sound like it doesn't bother me.

Rocco scowls. "You know she had us all enchanted with your magic," he says. "No way would I touch a Bella if I was in my right mind. I should have known something was up the second I started considering it."

"I'm glad to hear that," I admit.

"Why's that?" Rocco asks, raising an eyebrow. "You saying you want to be my girlfriend instead?"

"That might come with expectations I'm unable to fulfill," I say as we reach my door.

"Inevitable," he reminds me as I turn the key and step inside.

Peering out from inside, I see three of the men I've come to care about so much. A little pang goes through me that Ryker isn't here. I vow to talk to him soon, but for now, I have more on my mind than Ryker, or how I secretly want all the guys with me the way they were today, except all the way, and with Darius involved.

"Can we talk a little more?" I ask the professor. "I'm a little shook up, and I want to be ready next time Lilith shows up."

"Sure," he says, nodding and stepping into my room. I smile at the other two, give them a flirty wave, and close the door.

"What do you want to know?" Darius asks, pulling me back to reality.

"Where did she come from?" I ask, pacing back and forth. "Did she go back there? To the underworld?"

"My guess is yes, she returned to the spirit world," he says.

"And she wants to drag me down there with her," I say. "Does that mean I'll be dead?"

Darius frowns. "Not necessarily, but it can be very dangerous for mortals for obvious reasons."

"And we have no idea when she'll return."

"I'm sorry," he says, stuffing his hands in his pockets.

I stop in front of him. "Why do you do that?"

"Do what?" he asks, looking confused.

"You always look so uncomfortable around me," I say. "Are you making your hands busy so you won't touch me?"

His Adam's apple bobs as he swallows. "I don't think that's relevant."

"It's relevant to me," I say, stepping closer to him. I know he's been resisting this, but we've been dancing around it all year.

"Jade…" He says, but his hands fall on my hips when I step even closer, leaving only a whisper of space between us.

"Tell me you weren't even a little bit jealous when those guys were touching me," I whisper, my lips skimming over the stubble on his chin. "Tell me you didn't want to touch me again, too."

"I did," he admits, his eyes falling closed. "But…"

"But nothing," I whisper. "You can touch me."

"You're half my age."

I slide my hand behind his neck, my body coming alive at the touch of his skin. "Kiss me."

Darius opens his eyes, searching my gaze. "This is dangerous, Jade. I shouldn't be alone with you."

"I won't tell," I whisper, letting my hand rest over his hammering heart.

With a soft groan, he lets his lips meet mine. I melt against him, parting my lips and letting his tongue enter. As Darius kisses me, something inside comes alive, a crackling energy, a pulsating heat coursing through my veins. It rises in my chest, moving through my limbs, warming my fingers and toes, making everything tingle.

"Take me to the bed," I whisper.

Darius's arms wrap around me, and he lifts me off my feet and strides to the bed, laying me down and fitting his body on top of mine.

"Remember what I showed you," he reminds me.

With no more words between us, Darius kisses me slowly, passionately. Something deep in my core is waking up, a magical power, an essence that I didn't know I possessed until he unlocked it.

I wrap my legs around his hips, grinding my clit against the hard length of his cock. I need him inside me, need this power unleashed. I arch up, but he pins me to the bed, rocking against me.

"More," I whisper. But I know that no matter how much magic I have, he has more. He won't be swayed. His hands pinning mine to the bed tells me he's the one in control.

He won't give me more than this. One day, I'll make him lose control, but not tonight. Tonight I'm too far gone. My whole body is hot and aching for him. His mouth drops to my neck, leaving kisses, chasing shivers over my sensitive skin. Every nerve in my body comes more alive with each kiss, every touch. A need burns inside me like nothing I've ever felt before, and I feel the combination of my own power with my magic. It's addictive. I drive my wetness against Darius's shaft until I find the perfect rhythm. Pleasure builds inside me until I can't hold back. As I find release, I feel stronger, more powerful than I've ever felt before. And I love it.

Maybe being a sex goddess won't be so bad after all.

James & Phoenix

More Books by Alexa B. James

Academy of Sorcery Series (complete, also on audio)

-Term One: Unleashing Trials

-Term Two: Fallen Master

-Term Three: Shadow Magic

-Term Four: Secret Power

Cursed Throne Saga (complete, also on audio)

-Broken Princess

-Captive Princess

-Hunted Princess

-Fallen Princess

Rejected Mate Series (complete, also on audio)

-Banished From the Pack

-Shunned By the Pack

-Return to the Pack

Coyote Ranch Series (complete)

-Rope Me, Cowboys

-Wrangle Me, Cowboys

-Ride Me, Cowboys

-Wreck Me, Cowboys

-Wrap Me, Cowboys (Christmas novella)

This series is available in a complete series box set

Silver Shifter Series (complete, also on audio)

-Her Wolf

-Her Dragon

-Her Bear

-Her Panther

This series is available in a complete series box set

More Books by Athena Phoenix

Clash of Queens

-Prequel

-Tempting the Huntress

Boys of Summer

-Merlot

-Something Wicked

-The Naughty List

www.ingramcontent.com/pod-product-compliance
Lightning Source LLC
Chambersburg PA
CBHW032239010726
47494CB00002B/547